THIS BOOK IS FULL OF BODIES

RICK WOOD

BLOOD SPLATTER PRESS

ABOUT THE AUTHOR

Rick Wood is a British writer born in Cheltenham.

His love for writing came at an early age, as did his battle with mental health. After defeating his demons, he grew up and became a stand-up comedian, then a drama and English teacher, before giving it all up to become a full-time author.

He now lives in Loughborough, where he divides his time between watching horror, reading horror, and writing horror.

ALSO BY RICK WOOD

Chronicles of the Infected
Zombie Attack
Zombie Defence
Zombie World

Non-Fiction
How to Write an Awesome Novel
Horror, Demons and Philosophy

1

I AM a human in a monster costume, given to me by society.

But it's invisible.

No one can see it, not even me.

Every day I get up and I dress like one of you, except better. I talk like you except about more interesting things and I eat like you except my food costs more than you're worth.

I am you but a better you.

Because I don't deny my nature.

Think of all the constraints you place on yourself: monogamy, self-control, trust.

You deny what we are and tell me I'm weird because society has told you that and you're too stupid to question it.

I don't pretend to be like you, you just assume I am. You have your first glance at me, make your judgement, and then stick to it with the kind of stubbornness that shows why the human race is so deplorable.

I have this image, you see, and that image is faultless, and that's what makes it so easy. I live with Lisa, my wife, who I couldn't care less about. It's all part of the perfect family portrait. Me, Lisa, and...

Ah, yes. I forgot to mention.

I also live with Lisa's daughter.

Glorious sixteen with blowjob lips.

She's called Flora, like the butter.

I am wealthy as fuck, too.

I have seven businesses I inherited from my dead dad and I don't bother with any of them—I just let them earn my money and I spend it.

Lisa does not know it though.

I won't announce my fortune until she's dead.

I don't want her hands on it, and I need her to think I'm at work during the day, and not grinding some soon-to-be-deceased-eager-dick-chaser by a jukebox in a shitty pub three hours from anywhere she would think to look.

I have never killed before now. This may surprise you, considering the vivacious claim within the title of this book—but there would be little point in me starting the story after all the interesting stuff has already happened.

I mean, I've wanted to, of course I have.

I was fourteen when my geography teacher shouted at me and humiliated me in front of my class. I came in the next day and poured bleach into her coffee. A fat kid knocked it over her computer, and she shouted at him for being dangerous around electricity, claiming he could have killed her, never knowing that the fat lump of shit saved her life. That was the day I learnt what irony was. It was also the day I pissed on a cheeseburger and made an obese, tubby, lump of lard eat it, the fat fuck, for messing up what I wanted to do. I would have killed him too, but I didn't want to drag his fat fucking body around and try to squeeze it into acid or whatever fucking way you dispose of a body.

I hadn't quite learnt how to rid myself of a corpse yet.

I have, however, since learned about the nature of pigs,

and how they will eat anything. Now I know what to do when I eventually need to dispose of a body.

And it seems like here, dear reader, my ever-present voyeur, at about five hundred or so words in, it would be a good place to pause my memoir, just to check—am I offending you?

I mean, if talk of your stupid human nature and my succulent step daughter and of killing and bad fucking language and disposing of bodies of pathetic morsels with no purpose when you think about it in the grand existence of things does so offend you, I suggest you fuck off and find another book. I hear Pride and Prejudice is good for all you pansies looking for a quick thrill with no substance. Maybe you should return this book on your Kindle or phone or tablet or whatever device controls your useless little life nowadays and demand a refund. Return this book to a bookstore if you found one that actually had the audacity to sell it to you face-to-face.

I am not going to hold back, nor am I going to save myself from being honest in what I think, whether that be about me or what I do or about you, dear voyeur, you useless sycophantic stinking turd of a creature.

Go and give it a bad customer review on Amazon if you so wish; moan about how it was shocking and horrible, like the freedom to share your pointless opinion somehow validates that opinion, like what you have to say is something worth saying or worth listening to just because you can spread it across the internet.

But, if you would like to hear the true inner monologue of a fantastic beast of a man who does not deny his inner self and does not hold back in describing the delectable acts with which I do so engage, then read on—but do so knowing that to judge me would be to judge yourself.

"Ooh that's sick," and, "Ooh that's so wrong," and, "Ooh I

can't believe I just read that," only serves to show you are a true product of the feeble society that created you.

Whenever there have been no rules in society, there has been murder and mayhem. Little over a few hundred years ago people would flock to the arena to watch gladiators murder themselves and each other, much like you flock to your football stadiums now to see a less masculine show of testosterone.

Psychopaths have been needed by kings to do their duty in murdering those that need to be murdered.

But do not call me a psychopath.

And I request this for two reasons.

One, it shows you know little of what a true psychopath is. You would most likely go along with the Hollywood stereotype or the image created by true crime documentaries you binge watch on Netflix for 8.99 a month.

Two, it demeans what I do and makes it seem alien. It removes the human nature from human nature. It makes it seem as if what I do is unusual or not of the norm or is done because something is wrong with me.

As I said, gladiators killed and died for entertainment. People were hung for stealing in the 1800s and families would go watch it like the picnic in the park.

It is only recently that society has decided to find mindless and senseless acts of killing so unacceptable.

It is only now we don't pretend that we'd like to rip out the oesophagus of our impudent bosses, to tear the limbs from that arsehole hogging the middle lane of the motorway, or to stab that dickhead blocking the supermarket aisle with their trolley.

Because it is *wrong.*

Well, as you know, wrong is invented by your world. Wrong is only seen as wrong because you're told it's wrong.

Do what you feel.

Do what you want.

There is no heaven or hell for you to fear. Religion is ridiculous and don't even get me started on those fucking hypocrites who run the church.

I say this all not to shock you but to be straight with you; that I do not wish to have to censor what I do when I record it in this magnificent memoir of perfection. I wish to share every little detail and share it with all the satisfaction with which I do it.

So fuck off and read Jane Eyre if you've got a problem with it.

If you are ready to understand your true side, your true feelings, your true desires, then read on.

You may learn something.

Just don't pretend you are better than me.

I repeat:

Do not *ever* pretend you're better than me, you fucking cretin.

Pity the one who holds in their nature.

Envy the one who frees it.

2

————

MY TYPICAL DAY starts with the same tedious alarm, silenced by the same tedious wife. She rolls over; the covers draped below her thighs. She wears vest and pants. To most men this would be attractive. She is thin, mousy blond hair, and although she has cellulite on her cheeky little arse cheeks she owns it, she's confident with it, and that's so much more attractive than someone who just moans and moans about their shit body.

Truth is though, I'm bored.

If this was the first time I was seeing her then I wouldn't be able to wait to slide those panties off and pin her arms down and fuck her as I looked at the cactus on the windowsill and fantasise about choking her on it.

But, honestly, I don't want to touch her. Her body is sticky with sweat, and her mum scar—despite being sixteen years old—seems to light up in the morning sun. I thought it was sexy dating someone ten years older than me, but in truth, it was a phase. Like Tamagotchi's or pogs or nu-metal music, the spark just goes and you want something newer, something fresh.

I peel myself out of bed before she breathes her morning breath over me and asks for morning sex. She tries to entice me back to bed but I pretend I don't hear her and I go into the bathroom and I shit with the door open in hope this will mean she doesn't touch me. She does though. She strokes my neck as she comes in and begins brushing her teeth and oh aren't we the image of a married couple, shitting and brushing together.

I pretend I need to shit more just to get some peace. She goes downstairs and I hear the kettle boil just as I hear a bedroom door opening from down the hallway. I end my fake bowel movements and walk into the hallway.

There she is.

Standing in the doorway to her room.

Flora. Pouty lips, dainty waist, and tiny tits. I love tiny tits. The tinier the better. I love something I can grab in one hand and pretend it's been ripped off. She shaves, too. Usually girls her age have only just acquired their hair and aren't in such a rush to get rid of it, but she's the exception.

"Hey," she says, her voice sultry like silk.

I smile.

She walks past me to the bathroom. Her buttocks throb from side to side beneath pyjama shorts so miniscule that I can see everything. She leaves a gap in the bathroom door while she pees. I listen. I picture it.

She flushes and walks out.

"Can you stop staring at me?" she says.

"Right you are," I say, and walk sideways to the stairs so she can see my erection.

Downstairs, Lisa has her suit on and she's wearing trousers with a blazer. She dresses like a man. Sometimes women trying to be strong women do that. Don't get me wrong, I like strong women, but I disagree that a strong woman should dress like a man to appear as a strong woman. Why can't femininity be strong?

"Have you got a busy day today?"

"Yes," I say. "I've got the Anderson account and I might be late."

There's no Anderson and there's no account and there's no being late. I'm filthy rich, and she doesn't know it, but I'll be going to have a beautiful lunch she could never afford, followed by an afternoon of whatever I fancy. I'll be late because I'll probably be tying up a whore and inspecting their body with a flashlight.

Flora walks in. Now she knows how to dress. She dresses up like all those girls her age, with a skirt halfway between her waist and her knees that flows and brushes up in the breeze as she walks. The top three buttons of her school shirt are undone, and her blazer is hung over the strap of her shoulder bag. Her school socks are white and floral and go up to her knees. There's something so sexy about a knee between socks and skirt. In other circumstance a knee would just be a knee, but when it's framed in such a way it is immensely alluring.

"Right," Lisa says. "I am off. Have a good day at school."

She kisses Flora on the cheek. Flora doesn't react.

"Have a good day at work."

She kisses me on the cheek. I don't let her see me flinch.

"I should be back about five," she says. "When will you be home?"

"Late."

"Flora's got a parent's evening at seven, don't forget you said you'd come."

Ah, yes. A parent's evening for a teenage girl who's not my daughter. Wonderfuckingful.

"I'll be there."

Her heels make that irritating cloppy sound as they disappear into the distance, and she makes the house shake under the strength of her opening and shutting the door.

Me and Flora just look at each other.

She butters her toast, repeating the same action again and again as she just stares at me.

Either it's a cheeky little smirk or a knowing smile of loathing. I can never tell.

I convince myself that she wants me.

"Your mum will be back at five," I say.

"She is," she says.

"I'll be back about three thirty," I say.

"You will," she says.

She finishes buttering then scrapes the remnants of the plate into the bin.

"You not going to eat that?" I ask.

"I hate toast. I hate breakfast. I didn't want any. Just didn't want Mum going on about how important breakfast is."

Defiant little bitch.

I love it.

"Have a good day at school," I say.

"Oh," she says. "I will."

She walks out of the room, her skirt outlining the top of her posterior, swaying from side to side and I marvel at it the way cavemen once marvelled at the first wheel; something new to the world that will be used over and over.

I finish the shit coffee Lisa buys and I walk out the house and get into my Mercedes. I drive for about an hour until I get to a new restaurant that's being opened by some loud-mouthed chef from television. It's supposed to be expensive, which means it should be good. I go in and I order a coffee and already I can taste the difference between the exquisite bitter aroma of a marvellous cup of fresh beans and the

9

putrid vile Lisa purchases from whatever local chain of cheap food supermarkets she shops in.

"Would you like to see the brunch menu?" a waitress with stubby legs and high cheek bones asks.

"Veal. I want veal. I'm feeling veal—do you have any veal?"

"Erm, it's not on our brunch menu–"

"That isn't what I asked."

"I—I think we have some. I can go check."

"Yes, you do that."

That was more complicated than it needed to be.

I await her return with impatient anticipation. The napkin is folded into a duck. I pick up the fork and I stick it through the duck's neck, twisting it until it unfolds, and the duck lies as a dead piece of white fabric.

"The chef says he can do you some veal," she says, returning to my side before I notice she's there.

"Good," I say, not sure what else she's waiting for.

"Is there anything else you would like?"

"Well, what comes with the veal?"

"Creamed mashed potato, I think, an assortment of steamed vegetables doused in herbs, and–"

"All of that sounds fine."

She scuttles away like a lopsided beetle and I take a moment to myself. All around me are groups of people together on their mobile phones, living life through deadening technology. I don't have a mobile phone with me because I wish to experience life. I could kill all these people and they would be just the same as they are now. Dormant and alone. Pathetic and obsessed.

One of them takes a photo of their food. No, my dear, you are meant to eat it, not capture its image in the immortal hard drive of your coma-inducing device.

Pathetic. Sad. Really, all of them.

After eight minutes and thirty-two seconds my veal arrives and whilst I appreciate its speed it makes me sceptical as to how it was cooked.

I eat, satisfied that I am living a grand life whilst Lisa is not. It gives me a little tingle to know she will never get to experience what it's like to eat real food. Later on, I will chomp on the shit she makes before leaving most of it to the knapsack. Then I will imagine in what way it would be best for her die.

3

I SPEND my afternoon sat in a local bar with three people I call friends in an attempt to appeal to the world's requirement for someone normal to be surrounded by idiotic specimens they supposedly like. Having these pricks around makes it seem like I'm one of them, one of the guys, but they simply allow me to conform to conventions that make me seem *regular*.

There are three of them, all filthy rich and ugly as shit. Charles, Carter and Clayton. All names that begin with C, linking to how they all adhere to the connotations of another word beginning with C.

Charles dresses in a brown suit that looks like it's made from wool but probably isn't. He grows a moustache to try to hide the fact that he looks like he's still twelve, despite being thirty-two. The moustache looks like the kind of moustache a twelve-year-old Indian boy could grow. He sits back and crosses his legs and I wonder how small his dick and balls must be to do that. He has a wife, but he never talks about her, nor does he converse about his three daughters. There isn't even a picture of them in his wallet. It's like they don't even exist which, to Charles, they may as well not.

Carter is the quiet one. He likes to pretend it's because he's introverted and doesn't like idle chatter. Honestly, it's because he's too thick to say anything useful and too self-conscious about how thick he is to have the confidence to give his contribution to the conversation. He sits there every day, fingers clasped, desperately lonely. His seven-year-old son wants nothing to do with him, and how much of a sack of shit must you be for a seven-year-old to already realise you are a sack of shit?

Clayton is the kind of male you get in every male group. Sometimes you get more than one. He attempts to be the alpha male yet is anything but. He brags about his sexual conquests in the most vulgar of language but is probably getting the least sex out of all of us. Charles is married, so he is sure to have the obligatory fuck when it gets too long since he and his wife last fucked and they have to resign to the idea that they should probably fuck again. Carter may be quiet-mouthed and inept, but he has enough money to pay for whores—usually the same whore he keeps going back to, probably to convince himself he's in a relationship with her, despite him fucking her hours after she has likely fucked someone else. I even fucked her once, just for the fun of it, just so when he was fucking her and pretending to be in love I could have the knowledge he was enduring my sloppy seconds.

But Clayton, who is single—or a bachelor, living it up in his bach-pad as he calls it, a fifth four flat with a large glass wall overlooking the shitty parts of London (as if there are any other parts)—claims that he goes out most nights and picks up women; or *birds*, as he so chauvinistically calls them; I hate the term, it's demeaning to the avian population who grace our sky. A bird flies majestically overhead; a woman uses you and leeches off you until she's had enough to convince herself she is pretty.

Anyway, Clayton. He claims he has another *broad* every night—yes, he even uses that term too. *Broad*. As if we are in a 1940s film noir and he is the antihero getting seduced and manipulated by a femme fatale. In truth, his evening probably comprises him masturbating over expensive lesbian porn.

"So I had her down on the table," Clayton is saying, trying to make his voice sound cockney, as if that's how one speaks with the lads, despite the fact he comes from Northampton. "And I was like, bitch, do not break that table. It's worth more than you."

The others laugh so I do to. I see how Charles' body kind of convulses, like the shoulder pads of his suit jacket move up and down as he chuckles. I make mine do the same.

"What about you, Carter?" Clayton asks, and nudges Carter, who looks away. "You been getting any?"

Carter mumbles something we can't hear then lifts his bourbon with ice and sips on it.

"How's business going, Gerald?" asks Charles, turning to me.

I'd be fucked if I know. I do nothing with it but receive the checks.

"Very well," I tell him, attempting to mimic the intonations of his voice. "Business is going... very well. And yourself?"

I ask him how his business is doing because you're supposed to do that; feign interest in the lives of those that feign interest in yours. I have to stop myself from zoning out during his answer just in case he asks me about it later.

"Oh, brilliant, brilliant!" Charles declares. "We have just

had a successful merger with a stationery shop downtown. We now own them and are redesigning and rebranding."

"Wonderful!" Clayton declares.

"Yes, wonderful!" I say, stressing the same O vowel that Clayton does. Clayton smiles and nods vigorously in Charles' direction, so I do the same.

That's why I have these people in my lives, really. So I can look at how they act to know how I should act. If they didn't have such a function I would discard them completely.

It is at this point I realise I have half an erection and that the waitress looks quite attractive.

"Yes, it was trying at times," Charles said. He clicks his fingers to the waitress who comes over. "Another whiskey, please."

I click my fingers at the waitress just like Charles did.

"Another whiskey, please," I tell her.

She smiles a smile I know is not real, takes our glasses away and returns minutes later with another whiskey.

It's good stuff. Not the whiskey you'd buy off the shelves in your supermarket. Very occasionally you may find a bottle in one of those shops dedicated entirely to whiskey, but if you enter such a shop, it always seems to put you in the same vicinity as one of those hairy men who dwell in the dark corners of Wetherspoons all day with muddy boots and body odour you can smell across the store—so I'd rather have the whiskey here. It costs more than Lisa's weekly shop does all together and I look forward to when I don't have to pretend this isn't the life I love to live.

"... and Hector told me it couldn't be done..." Charles is still talking. "... well I say to hell with you, old chap, there is not a chance I am walking away from this one..."

I tune out again, but a little later Clayton claps and laughs so I do the same, coinciding my sip of whiskey with his.

And I tune them out again and look at the waitress. You can see the outline of her thighs squeezed into her fitted skirt and I imagine just reaching my hand up there and grabbing her.

"... and I said I'd be damned if I know!"

Another laugh and I join in.

I always join in.

Even if I don't necessarily fit in.

I LIKE

I LIKE when my favourite TV show is on—but not just as scheduled; when I turn on the TV and there is a repeat of one of my favourite episodes.

It makes me just sit back and think... I am one lucky girl.

I like the way Disney shaped my years growing up, but never turned me into a dainty little princess. I never wanted to be the princess, I wanted to be the warrior; I wanted to be fierce like a dragon and drive every bully and teacher away.

I like beans on toast.

I like drama lessons, especially ones where we get to improvise, or create a play from a script.

My favourite script is called 4:48 Psychosis. It was written in 2000 by a playwright called Sarah Kane. She wrote it whilst she was sectioned, then killed herself afterwards.

It's extremely morbid.

But it's also so unconventional, and in that way, I can relate.

It is not written as a play would. There is no indication who says what. Lots of the words aren't even indented properly. Sometimes there are scenes where lines have bullet points, but it's open to interpretation.

There is no set way to perform it.

But then I got too into the performance, and me and my friends pretended to slash our wrists and painted our skin in with red markers that wouldn't wash off and it made us late for textiles.

Our drama teacher never did that play with us again.

Funny though, how no one thought to ask why there was a faint colouring of red at the end of my arm.

I like how I get to be myself.

I like how I can express myself and mum and my stepdad just accept it.

Although, sometimes, I think if my mum asked questions, she'd get to know the real me. She'd learn what really happens when she's not looking.

And that scares me.

...

...

...

I like the moon. Not just in a 'look at me I'm a free spirit' annoying kind of way. I just like when it's dark but the moon is lit, especially a full moon, when they say all the crazies come out.

But I'm not crazy.

I just like to sit on my windowsill and watch it and feel at peace and know that everything is all right. Despite what worries and trials I may face at school or at home, I can just look into the sky and know that it is all too small to matter.

Most people don't enjoy hearing that they don't matter.

And they don't, when you think about how many forms of life have existed, and not just on our planet.

But it makes me feel content.

I like to know that, no matter what I endure, there is no reason to it. It doesn't scare me that there is no purpose to it all, like it does all those spiritual answer-seekers.

I like knowing that when it all ends, all the mistakes I have done will leave with me.

I like knowing that it will end, someday.

I like knowing that there will be a day when I will not cry anymore.

...

...

...

I like when we do practical in science. I sit by Pierre, who has come from France to live here and doesn't speak much English. He still smiles though, and sets up the Bunsen burner, and we need not say much to know what the other is thinking and we work together so well.

I like Pierre.

I like being young, although I don't feel young anymore. I feel like my youth is gone. Taken from me.

Maybe it was.

But it was all my fault, really.

It's always my fault.

They say an adult owns up to their mistakes and accepts them, and that is why I feel so much older than everyone else around me.

No one at school mentions sex, unless it's sharing what they have done. Some of them have kissed, some of them have fiddled with their hands, some of them have even seen someone topless.

For me, I just stay quiet in those conversations.

I like keeping things to myself.

I like the secret being hidden away.

I like to pretend that I am just like them, and I know nothing about it, and it's all new and exciting, and that I do not have a vast sexual history.

I like to cry sometimes, too.

...

...

...

And I like Gerald.

Honestly, I do.

I mean it.

Really.

I like him.

I just don't like what he does to me when he gets home.

4

WHEN I ARRIVE HOME at three thirty-six, she's already waiting for me on the sofa. She spreads her pubescent legs from one side to the other, revealing white knickers with something on them. Beas, I think. Maybe flowers. Who gives a fuck?

"Good day at school?" I ask.

"Yes."

I walk toward her. She flinches back.

"What are you doing?" I demand.

"I—can we do it differently today?"

This again.

Fuck sake.

Every few days it's the same old shit. She wants to try *making love* and she wants to try *slow and steady* and if I don't listen to her and acquiesce her request, she'll tell her mum and then I say go tell her, see what she says when her daughter claims she fucked her husband. See who they think is the crazy one, me or her.

"Please, Gerry, can we just–"

"It's Gerald."

I fucking hate it when she calls me that. She thinks it's

sweet, like she has a name that only she calls me, and that makes this special. She overestimates the value of what we do.

I walk toward her and she closes her legs and backs away. It angers me and arouses me at the same time.

"I just thought it would be nice if–"

I jump on her and land my legs either side of her knees and I grab her wrists in my hands and lift them behind her head.

"If you want to do this, then we have to do it in a way that makes us both–"

I shush her. It sounds like she's being doing some kind of relationships education at school and they've been told all about their rights. It'll pass.

"Please," she says.

I lean my head down and bite her neck then run the bottom set of my teeth upwards to her ear where I bite until she flinches away.

"I just want to–"

I put both of her wrists into one hand and use the other to cover her mouth. Her voice is muffled, and she moves her head out of it and she looks at me in the same way her mum does when she's cross and realises I couldn't care less.

"Just today, can we–"

I take off my sock and I shove it in her mouth and she tries to spit it out but I already have the gag in my pocket ready and I tie it around her mouth and I had the rope ready and she tries to resist—it's all part of the game—and I bind her hands.

She crawls away and whimpers and I jump onto her back and I love this part. She cries and I ignore her and I tie the rope around her wrists and leave enough of the rope that I can pick her up and drag her around which I do. I don't put her in any place, I just walk her by the makeshift lead around the leaving room. She looks up to me and her mascara is smudged because her eyes are moist. She shakes her head and makes a noise like she's pleading and it's still all just part of the game.

I let go of the rope and she stands and she tries to run away. She tries to get to the front door, but it's locked and she looks for the key but she won't find it.

I walk toward her and she doesn't move. She looks at me and pleads with her eyes. I grab her hair and I bend her over the table and I rake up her skirt and I pull down her pants and my god her rear end is just damn perfect.

I slide myself in and she tries to lift her head and I slam it onto the table and hear her wince with the impact.

I fuck her hard and she screams and I'm not sure if it's part of the game or if she's cumming or if I'm hurting her or if it's all three but I cum quicker than I intended and then I stop, just bent over her, breathing into her ear.

I sit down on the floor, leaning against the door. She falls to her knees and looks away from me.

I pat the floor next to me and she looks to me like a wounded animal and I pat it again. She moves and sits there.

I take the gag off and remove the sock but I leave her hands tied.

She leans her head on my shoulder.

We say nothing for a while.

Eventually, I release her hands, and we stay there, in that position. Content and happy. The way one is after an orgasm. Honestly, I reckon politicians should all fuck before parliament so their heads are clearer and they make better decisions.

"It really hurt that time," she says.

"What?"

"It really hurt."

"It's supposed to hurt."

"No, I mean, I was too dry. There was no foreplay or anything."

I shrug. Who gives a fuck?

"Maybe it would be nice if we didn't tie me up. Just one time. Just to see what it's like."

I move her head off my shoulder and I look at her. She is a state. Her skirt is still riding up her belly from where I hiked it up. She has leaked cum on the floor.

"I thought you liked it like this?" I say. "I thought you enjoy our game?"

"I do, really, I do." She lifts her hand and strokes my face, then leaves it at my chin. She gives me a soft, delicate kiss. Why does she always need to do this afterwards? What we do is awesome, it's fucking amazing, but she always needs this crap after.

"I like tying you up. Do you not like me tying you up?"

"I love it, you know I do."

"Then quit moaning."

"I'm not, it's just..."

I stand. I huff.

"Please don't go!" she begs. "Mum will be back in an hour and we don't have much time."

"I said I'll be late. I have to go before she gets back."

She pushes herself to her feet and her legs wobble and she uses my body to steady her.

"I miss you when you're gone."

You miss me when I'm gone?

I ignore her. I get the spray and the kitchen roll and clean the cum off the floor. She gets the rope and the gag and she takes it to her room where she hides it. The same routine.

I double check for evidence. There's a little bit of blood on the chair next to the table. I don't know if that was us, so I clean it up, anyway. Just in case.

I'm halfway out the door when she appears on the bottom step.

"Don't forget about the parent's evening later."

"Yes, yes, yes, I know."

"I will not be home after school tomorrow," she tells me. "You'll have to find something else to do with your afternoon. I have dance class."

I scoff. "Dance class?"

"Yeah. It's something I'm trying out. Like a hobby."

"I am your hobby."

"Like a real hobby."

I look her up and down. She'd look sexy dancing. If she did it right. Otherwise, she'd look pathetic.

I shrug and leave.

Why would I care?

5

I DRIVE AROUND for the next hour or so wondering what to do with my last hour of freedom. And it is freedom, before you say I am being dramatic—the only time I can be liberated from the person Lisa expects me to be and Flora pretends I am. The only time I can breathe without those two girls chatting like they are in some kind of sitcom awaiting the canned laughter. They think they are funny because they laugh together and there is a difference between actually being funny and being caught inside a bubble with another person where the only people who find you funny are contained within.

I stop outside Carluccio's and let the valet take my car, watching him as he drives it around the corner, knowing that if he swings those wheels too hard or jars the gear stick I will break his twiggy legs. As soon as I am inside, they take my jacket and welcome me in.

"Is Carluccio in today?" I ask the woman at the counter. I recognise her from the last few times I ate here. She was new but now I guess she's not. She has a layer of makeup on that changes her skin colour and it makes me want to slap her until she stops trying to cover up her actual, real, true beauty. Acne scars are beautiful. Wrinkles are beautiful. Birth marks are beautiful. Covering it up with artificial substances to the point it makes you look like you're some weird yellow ethnicity that doesn't exist just highlights to everyone else around you how damn insecure you are. Be confident with your body, because if you menially try to change it so much everyone will know what you really think of yourself.

"Yes, he is," she says, and I can't tell if that's her real voice or if it's as fake as her face. It's low and husky like she has a cold or is trying to put on some sexy voice that doesn't work.

"Wonderful. Can you send him over to take my order?"

"I think he's busy."

"Tell him it's Gerald. He'll come. I'll sit at my usual table."

I can't talk to her any longer, so I walk through the restaurant between tables of couples pretending to love each other and friends appeasing each other's jokes with over-psyched fake hysteria until I find my seat by the window. I sit and put the napkin on my lap and look at the wineglass. I pick it up and look inside. I can see a slight smear from where the dishwasher tab did not quite dissolve.

"Can I get you any–"

"Yes," I say. I don't even bother to look up as she finishes her question. "You can get me a new glass. One without this shit in it. And you can get Carluccio to bring me out some Pavillon Blanc du Château Margaux."

Bordeaux do make nice wines.

She scuttles away saying nothing else, of which I am grateful for. After roughly a minute and a half Carluccio comes out with his arms out wide.

"Gerald!" he says, extending the vowels of my name—this means he's pleased to see me. He's wearing his chef outfit and chef hat and he's podgy and has a huge bit of

27

waddle beneath his chin that shakes when he talks but damn I like this guy. There are very few people I tolerate but Carluccio is *the guy.* Not only does he serve the best fucking salmon I ever allowed into my mouth, he is always pleased to see me and tells all his waitresses to treat me well.

I stand and I pretend to kiss one cheek then the other but I don't actually put my face on his because I like him but I don't want to smudge my cheek and have to keep washing it until I feel clean again.

"How are we today?"

By *we* he means *me,* but for some reason he likes to use an inclusive plural. I suspect this is to create some sort of unification, or perhaps a feeling of empathy.

"I am well, Carluccio, I am well," I tell him, doing that thing when I repeat the answer twice either side of his name, like a sandwich where my answer is the bread and his name is the big wad of ham.

"I am delighted to hear this!"

He always speaks with an Italian accent that I can't quite tell whether is fake or not.

"What are you drinking today?" he asks.

"I am having some of the lovely Bordeaux wine."

"Excellent!" He turns behind him and claps his hands together to get the waitress's attention. "Where is that Pavillion Blanc, my dear girl?"

She frowns like she's being condescended to and how dare she frown at such a wonderful boss as Carluccio. There is a blender behind her and I wonder how quickly I could remove her hand if I shove it in there and grind it off.

"And how is the family?"

Carluccio doesn't know my family, but he always seems to ask this.

"They are well," I say, never wanting to reveal what family I have. I adamantly keep these two lives separate.

"I am glad to hear this!"

He is always so glad and enthusiastic and happy and I really do like this chap.

"I would recommend the linguine today," he says. "I have just made it fresh. It is exquisite."

"Then I will have the linguine."

This is where I fill up on real food before I go home and pretend to like the shit Lisa makes. Sometimes she asks me to make tea but I won't because, what, you think I will make tea when I never actually eat home-cooked food? This way I can scrape most of her preposterous culinary disaster into the bin and I will never go hungry.

"I must get back to the kitchen," says Carluccio, and I am saddened to hear this. "But I do hope you enjoy your pasta. Let me know what you think!"

"Thank you, I will, thank you, Carluccio."

He leaves. The waitress who gave Carluccio the grimace brings over my wine and I give her the same look she gave him.

"Hey," I say.

"Can I help you?" she asks with a voice that sounds like she's trying to be friendly but a face that says she would rather be anywhere than doing this job, serving me.

"I didn't like that."

"Didn't like what?"

The stink-eye you stupid fuck.

"You know what."

She looks confused. Pretends she doesn't understand.

"Okay..." she says and tries backing away.

But I grab her wrist and she is not going anywhere.

"Do it again and I will rip your trachea up through your

larynx, out your trap, then shove it back in knowing it's still not the filthiest thing that's been in there."

I look at her so she knows I mean it. She looks confused and terrified and intimidated all at the same time and that little spark of fear that makes the arm I grab shake gives me a little tingle.

"Now fuck off."

She shuffles away and I can hear her crying but she covers it up so no one sees and she will never fuck with Carluccio again.

I let it go and sip my wine and wow that is good wine.

Bordeaux do good wines.

6

It's the time of day where everyone has their lights on without their curtains closed.

As if early evening is a time to give voyeurs permission to do what they do.

I return home at eighteen minutes to seven. Lisa is sat at the table waiting for me. She is wearing the same business suit she was wearing this morning. This means she hasn't showered or changed. This means when she peels away the sweaty layers of clothing later I am going to have to suffer that push of odour that wafts from her once appealing naked body toward my always suffering nostrils.

Flora is next to her.

She has changed out of her school uniform, which is a shame, but then again, it isn't. I can't spend the evening imagining raking up that wafting skirt. Luckily, she has chosen to wear trousers. The kind that young people wear that are practically sewn onto their legs. You can make out all the curves but not in a flattering way. It will help to keep my attentions curbed throughout the monotony of this evening.

"Where have you been?" Lisa asks. She tries to sound

authoritative, which would make me angry if she didn't instead come across as intensely whiny.

"What's the problem?" I ask. "Parent's evening is at seven."

"It's quarter to seven now!"

Actually, it has just turned seventeen minutes to seven. No need to exaggerate, you insufferable wretch.

"Well, that gives us plenty of time to get to a school which is, by my last reckoning, eight minutes away."

"But I want to be there before it starts to make sure we're on time."

Lisa thinks she has some profound concept of timekeeping, something that seems to make her fail to realise that out of the two of us I am the one who always keeps an appointment. I detest lateness, finding it to be the rudest of gestures; as if an individual expects everyone else to get there on time whilst this hypothetical imbecile—who owns a watch yet makes little use of it—can simply waltz in three minutes after the scheduled o'clock and expect instant redemption. It is not to be forgiven and is immensely deplorable and this is why it incenses me so that this drooping cow thinks she can ever ridicule my standards at timekeeping. If I ever plan to partake in an activity that involves her—something that would happen far more rarely should I have my way—I always provide her with an estimated time of arrival that is at least ten minutes before my desirable estimated time of arrival, knowing that she will believe that ten minutes is *nothing really so don't get so bent out of shape about it we can just go when we want there's no real time we have to arrive* in which case what is the fucking point of choosing a time that we will arrive in advance anyway.

"Shall we go?" I ask. "Or would you like to delay us further by debating the merits of timekeeping and who has the superior ability to look at a watch?"

"Really, Gerald," she says as she stands up and shoves the chair under the table with a gesture she probably thinks makes her seem scary but only marks the floor that I had to pay for. "I don't know why you–"

"Shut up," I tell her. "I am not interested."

She huffs and I turn away from her to avoid any further entanglement in words flung one way then the other. I open the door for her and let her pass through, which she does without a *thank you* or *you're so kind* or *I'm so sorry for being such a foul wife*. I hold it open for Flora too, who gives me a strange look, a shifty one, as if she's upset with me or so it seems. I give a cheeky grin and a little wink, and she just smiles.

I walk out to find Lisa standing beside my Mercedes.

"No," I say.

"Oh, come on, Gerald, we don't have time to argue about this."

I do not want her in my car.

It's just...

I do not want her in my car.

She will put her grubby little fingers on the dashboard and the sweat from her buttocks in the suit she's worn all day will seep through the seat, and no one will admit they can smell it but no end of fragrances I can acquire would ever remove it.

"Let's go in your car," I say.

"Gerald, please, would you just drive us there."

Oh and look who's getting her way again! I would recount the last time it was me who had things go their way in this marriage, but I would be here for far too long trying to recollect such an incident.

I slide into the driver's seat, watching through the generosity of my mirror as my glorious little minx slides into the seat behind me. Her hair falls down her shoulders and springs politely back up.

"Come on then, let's get a–"

I press *on* and a compact disc of some loud music starts at the high volume with which I was listening to it earlier, immediately interrupting her. The silence, albeit a silence obscured by heavy metal and screaming and distorted guitars, is a good one.

She presses the *on* button once more and the music turns off.

The driver is in charge of the car, and that includes the music. One should not overstep their boundaries and change the music without first gaining permission. This incenses me and I want to grab the back of her greasy mound and pound her head into the dashboard repeatedly, but would regret doing so as it would just create more mess from her facetious body that I would have to clean up, along with the sweat stains that are already beginning to form below her once-delectable buttocks.

We drive in silence to the school. At least, I do. Lisa turns around and starts nagging Flora about something. It's annoying, yes, but at least it is not me her irritating attention is now focussed on. I am quite content driving my car, trying to pretend she has not somehow found her way into it against my wishes.

Ten minutes later—meaning we get there a whole six minutes ahead of schedule, how's that for timekeeping you vapid, decrepit, little whore—we remove ourselves from the car and I intentionally do so without looking at the poor seat that had just suffered the perspiration of her anal pores.

The teachers are arranged across a few rooms. The first is called *the grand hall* but is barely a *moderate hall*. The second is a tiny library that stocks books like *Twilight*, providing all the reasons why literature should not be attempted by just anyone. The third and final room is a cafeteria that still smells like stale chips. The whole place stinks of lifeless children and tastes like lost dreams, and this is it, this is where ambition goes to die.

The first teacher is a man with a large moustache that resembles that of one Albert Einstein. He is her science teacher and introduces himself as Mr Albert and I scoff loudly at the irony.

I love irony. It is one of the few tacits of human nature that I seem to be able to understand. Unfortunately, that does not always stretch to sarcasm, and I often find myself confused in conversation with one who claims to have a wonderful sense of humour. To me, most people who think they have a wonderful sense of humour are the same as those people who say they are bubbly to disguise having to describe themselves as obese. After all, what person would not claim to have a wonderful sense of humour? It is a trait most believe they have acquired, yet very few actually have.

All the tables are set out with the teacher on one side and three chairs prepared on the other. Flora sits in the middle one, of course, Lisa sits to her left, and I sit on the right. I ignore Mr Albert and subtly peer through the corner of my eye at a teacher sat at the adjacent table. She is an overbearingly enthusiastic drama teacher who has pigtails I would just love to pull as I grind my crotch against her cheeks.

"Flora is a lovely girl," the man says, and she is not a *girl* she is a *woman*. She has breasts, does she not? Pubic hair, albeit that she removes upon my request? Childbearing hips and armpit hair that requires shaving?

Yes, she is not a girl; she is glorious sixteen, so don't speak of my Flora with such patronising language.

"She really excels at biology," he says, and I agree, particularly the part involving reproductive glands. "She enjoys chemistry, and physics is something she needs to work on."

He pauses, leaving his mouth open with an elongated verbal filler stuttering out of it, as if he is struggling to decide how to articulate his next sentence. I never understand why people do this. Just speak. Why create this amateur dramatic show where you feign hesitance to make it seem like you care about the effect of the words you are about to deliver?

"Flora can, however, er..." There he goes again, stretching out another *er* as if he will keep it going all evening. "Can, er... Well... She can er... Be a bit childish."

"Childish?" Lisa replies. Evidently, she was not expecting this. Neither was I.

"Yes," Mr Albert says, with a slow but large nod.

"In what way?" Lisa asks.

"She can often giggle at things she shouldn't giggle at. She says things that are inappropriate. Sexual things. And this is the back of her book."

He shuffled through some pages of a worn-out exercise book and I feel Flora shrink down in her seat as Mr Albert reveals a page of well-drawn cocks. They are of varying sizes, some are coloured in black and are larger than the others, which amuses me I have to say (although I get the feeling I'm not supposed to display that reaction), and a few lines have been used to draw pubic hair on the scrotal region. I try to identify my own penis among the drawings and wonder how Flora knows how so many penises look when she is so very used to just my own.

"Well, this is very immature," says Lisa. She glances at me as if she wishes for me to concur. I say nothing.

I glance at Flora. I want to snigger with her, but Lisa's glare tells me not to. Flora doesn't look at me.

The next teacher is a French teacher who is actually from

France and has some surname I can't pronounce and didn't particularly care enough to remember. She gives the usual niceties and encouragement and praise and then ends up saying something very similar. She even presents another page in Flora's exercise book with more penises, now with a few additional breasts and arses. One of the penises has a very well outlined beret on, and I can't see why the French teacher would be so annoyed about that when she is clearly adapting her phallic drawings for the subject in which she is studying.

We go onto PE who say that she says wildly inappropriate things in the dressing room and talks openly and grandly about sex, and then English say something similar about references to period blood in a Shakespeare play they are studying—regretfully, I failed to hear the name of the play, which is a shame as I like the eloquence of old William's language—and so maths also report similar grievances, claiming she was using the ruler to point out the average size of a man's genitals, which again is adapting her focus to the subject she is learning and I don't know what's so bad about that if it means it's relevant. History say the same thing and Geography and all the others and so forth, until we are done, and I am fed up and me and Lisa are stood alone outside the bathroom waiting for Flora to finish urinating.

"I don't understand," says Lisa.

"Don't understand what?" I ask, because that's what I'm supposed to do, isn't it? Pretend to care?

"Why she's so obsessed with sex."

"It is odd," I muse, gazing out at the window as I see that teacher with pigtails again.

"Do you think she's sexually active?" Lisa says, and she turns to me with a face I have come to assume is concern.

I say nothing.

"I mean, I know she's sixteen, and she's starting to like boys, and I know she must have kissed a boy or two, of course —but do you think she's doing more than that?"

"More than what?"

She seems to ignore the question, probably thinking it wasn't genuine.

"Maybe we should have a conversation with her."

We? It's your daughter.

"About what?" I ask.

"About sex. Contraception, relationships, that kind of stuff. What do you think?"

I shrug.

"What if we take her for a burger now? What if we go somewhere, congratulate her for so much positivity, and then we can ask her about all those doodles? It's not too late is it? I mean, it's Friday after all?"

She asks all these many questions then looks at me as if I'm supposed to know which one she wants answering.

"Yes," I say, hoping this will cover it.

"Wonderful!"

Flora comes out of the bathroom and Lisa tells her we're going to get a burger and I realise this will be at a greasy fast-food restaurant where the meal costs less than a small glass of sparkling water does at the kind of place I would wish to go to. What's more, we have to drive to the middle of nowhere surrounded by nothing but forest to get to her favourite fast food establishment.

Fuck.

I should have listened to those questions.

7

WE ARE SAT in one of the most repulsive locations I have ever entertained, surrounded by people who look like they should be bedbound or covered up. Greasy skin, obesity and mouths full of processed food surround me like a horde of zombies readying themselves to attack. They stuff their mouths with cheeseburgers and chicken nuggets which probably contain less meat than a vegetarian's shit. Their slomping mouths create the background ambience of this godforsaken hellhole, drowned out only by the tuneless electronic beat of something vaguely resembling music quietly pulsating out of poor-quality speakers.

Flora devours her burger like she has never eaten and it pains me to think I have entered that mouth. Lisa chew on hers with the daintiness of a mouse and I sit there, looking at the burger she has acquired for me, wondering how I can sneak it into the bin without being noticed.

"So," Lisa begins, and she already has her *mother voice* on. "We are both so proud of you for how well you've done, on the effort you are putting into your work. Aren't we?"

She looks to me and it takes me a while until I realise I am supposed to say something. In truth, I'm still distracted by the barely dead animal sandwiched between two poorly defrosted pieces of bread.

"Yes," I say, and look back to the deplorably poorly slain beast that constitutes one's dinner.

"We are, however, a little concerned about some of the, er... *sexual*... things you've been saying."

Why is she emphasising the word *sexual*? We are talking about sex and dicks and cunts and it doesn't really matter whether you place an emphasis that poorly disguises your discomfort or not, that is what we are conversing about.

Flora says nothing. She is already halfway through her burger and I can sense a burp coming and oh lord I hope it doesn't.

"What can you tell us about that?" Lisa asks.

Flora shrugs.

"Maybe we need to talk about sex. Do you know how to get a condom, for example?"

The family sitting a few seats across from us choke on their gherkin.

"Yes, I know how to get condoms."

"Good. And do you use them?"

"Do I use them?" she repeats, and I think she's angry.

"Okay, maybe that was a tactless way of asking it. I know you're growing up and you're not a child anymore, and if you aren't already, you will become sexually active soon, and, well, we just want to make sure you're okay."

Someone I recognise walks in through the door and I tune myself out of the conversation.

Who is it?

Then I realise.

It's Carluccio.

The normal warm pleasure I get at seeing this wonderful

man doesn't rise through my stomach. Instead, I am filled with dread and terror and like Macbeth *o full of scorpions is my mind...*

I try to look away but Carluccio has already seen me. He raises his arms in the air in a grand gesture Italian people seem to think everyone else appreciates, and he begins his walk toward me.

Lisa and Flora haven't seen him yet, they are too engaged in a heated conversation and I hear the words *boy* and *sex* and *condom* being repeatedly thrown about and I try to figure out how to get rid of this man but it's too late, he's here next to me and he's saying hello in a big grand gesture no one could miss.

"It is so good to see you!" he says. "And here with your family too!"

Lisa and Flora don't know I have money and no job and they can't know I have money and no job and Carluccio is going to ruin that and *fuck sake Carluccio.*

"I don't know you," I say, and it's too late, Lisa and Flora have already stopped talking and turned to listen.

"They are such pretty ladies, why don't you ever bring them to the restaurant, hey?"

"What restaurant?" Lisa asks.

I tell Lisa I'll be right back and I stand and I grab Carluccio's arm and I march him away and I glance back and they are already re-engaged in their heated debate about sex and penises and boys. By the time I get him outside I hope they have already forgotten him.

"Mr Brittle, have I done something–"

"Shut the fuck up," I tell him, speaking quickly and assertively although some people say my assertive voice sounds like my aggressive voice but it doesn't.

"I don't–"

"I said shut the fuck up, Carluccio, shut the fuck up. If you set foot in this shitty excuse for a restaurant I will force my fist so far down your throat I'll be able to grab your gullet. Get the fuck away from here, you understand?"

He looks back at me in stunned silence and I assume he has the idea, so I return inside and return to my seat, ready to give a lie as to who he was, but they don't care, they are amid a heated argument and are not interested.

"But why won't you tell me his name?" Lisa says.

"Because I don't want to!" Flora says.

"She has a boyfriend," Lisa tells me, "and she is refusing to tell me who he is, or even how she knows him."

Lisa has a boyfriend I think and I get mad with rage until I realise *I am the boyfriend* even though there is no point I have or ever would agree to be her *boyfriend* but she must have somehow referenced that she is sexually active with someone and Lisa has interpreted that as *boyfriend* and dear god she cannot tell Lisa it's me.

"Best to mind her privacy," I say.

"Oh, thanks a lot!" Lisa barks, and turns back to her daughter. "I think it's about right you tell me who he is, if he is dating my daughter."

"No, I don't think it matters."

Oh, please don't.

"I just want a name."

"No!"

No, please no.

"Just a name, that's it."

Flora leans back, she thinks, and she looks at me, and I beseech her with my eyes and she eventually turns to Lisa and says, "Fine."

Fuck.

"Well?" Lisa asks.

Fuck fuck fuck.

"You really need to know his name?"

"Yes, I do."

Fuck fucking fuck fucking fuck.

"Fine," she says, and I get ready to act, ready to do something, but then, to my astonishment, she says, "his name is Mark."

And... what?

Mark?

Who the fuck is Mark?

"And how do you know him?"

"I sit next to him in maths. We met up at break time and made out behind the bike sheds, if you really need to know."

Mark.

Fucking Mark.

I hate Mark.

Who the fuck does Mark think he is?

"And is it serious?"

Flora shrugs.

"Kinda. I meet up with him a few times after school."

"And how long have you and Mark been dating?" I ask.

"About three months."

Three months.

We've been fucking for longer than that which means that since she met me she's been fucking with this guy this *Mark* and I fucking *hate Mark* and I want *to kill Mark* and I will find out who he is and strangle him and–

Carluccio walks back into the store.

He glances at me timidly.

All my rage intensifies, my anger about Mark and my hatred of Mark and Mark Mark Mark Mark fucking Mark.

I stand and march toward Carluccio and he disappears outside and into an adjacent alley.

I step outside and look up and glance at the CCTV

43

camera. Someone who works in the fast food establishment walks past me so I quickly grab her attention and point to the camera.

"Excuse me, someone hit my car the other day, I was wondering if–"

"Oh, I'm sorry, those are just for show. We stopped bothering recording with them a few months ago. Nothing ever happens here."

"Thank you," I say and try not to grin as she walks on.

I march down the alleyway.

And the car park where my dear Mercedes dwells is right next to it.

"Please, Mr Brittle, I–"

I grab his throat and I shove him against the wall and I squeeze it so tight I can feel his pulse deaden and my thumb and finger throb, but it's too quick, way too quick, so I shove him against a dumpster and grab the back of his hair and lift his head back and soar it into the dumpster and back and into and back and into and back again until he's too groggy to run and I drop him to the floor.

There is a brick nearby so I pick it up and I mount him and he looks vaguely up at me and I drive the brick downwards.

Blood splashes over my coat which is so annoying as I love this coat but at least it keeps it off my suit and maybe I can get it dry cleaned but then again I won't want to be noticed as if the police go asking around they will say they cleaned blood off and there is blood on the dumpster I must deal with and this brick and oh boy I've been beating him with this brick the whole time and I was distracted and I do believe he is already dead.

8

I FEEL GUILTY.

I shouldn't have done it.

I was wrong.

That's what you want me to say, isn't it?

So I'll say it.

It was a terrible thing to do and I feel awfully bad and I hope this doesn't mean you don't like me anymore and I hope you will still keep reading this book because I would hate for it to be too violent for you and yada yada yada yada yada don't give a shit.

But I'll say it.

Anything that helps my fancy dress.

Anything that makes you feel comfort.

Comfort is the enemy of awareness.

And, as you sink further and further into security, that's when I'll get you. That is when you will be ripe for the pickin's, as they say.

I look around everywhere for witnesses, back and forth for anyone I may have to add to Carluccio's grave predicament, and I keep doing this as I back my car up. I step out inconspicuously and I open the boot once I have the car ready and I shove the body into it, as I do my coat, as I do the brick.

I have some Windowlene I used to clean my windows and some Tyrex I used to do my tyres and some car wash I used to do my car and it's not ideal but that will have to do.

With another glance I head back into the alley and look for obvious blood. There is no way for me to get rid of everything, but if they don't know where he was killed they won't know where to look for what they can't see. After all, there is none of my blood there.

With the CCTV not working, the main thing I need to get rid of is any forensic trace to me. That is the only thing they may have. Once the elements have attacked the surface, however, in the time they take to discover he's missing and inspect the alley, I should be fine.

I think I'll be fine.

I think.

I scrub at the side of the dumpster and the floor and the wall and it's the most manual labour I've done in my life and it hurts my back.

My phone rings.

It's Lisa.

Dammit.

I answer.

"Hey."

"Where are you? We're coming up to the car park and we can't see your car. Where did you go?"

They can't come into the car park.

They can't enter and see where I am and where my car is.

"Meet me outside the restaurant."

"The restaurant?"

"Uh huh. I'll just drive around and get you."

"But don't you–"

"Just meet me there."

I hang up.

Within five minutes the alleyway looks clear. No one is around and it's dark so I shine my phone light upon all the floors and sides and the dumpster and I hope there's rain tonight to help wash the invisible evidence away.

He won't be reported missing until at least tomorrow when he doesn't show for work; dependent upon, of course, whether he has a wife which is doubtful, he's too much of a podgy fuck for a woman to commit to fucking him for her whole life. Which means that any rain we get tonight will help and I get out my phone and look at the weather app and gosh am I in look—we are due thunderstorms *all night long.*

I am one lucky fucker.

I lock the boot and I don't know what I will do with him yet but I'm sure I'll think of something. I walk around to the driver's seat and I leave and there'll be a camera somewhere nearby that will have picked up the number plate of my car.

There were many cars that were in the car park at the time of his disappearance. Without little to go on, this may be the police's first line of enquiry. They may look for mine first, or they may look for it last. Either way, I can't risk them taking the chance to test the boot—his DNA will be all over it.

I need to get rid of it.

Which is a damn shame as it's a bloody nice car.

I pick up Lisa and Flora and they are continuing their conversation about Mark, this little fucking pip squeak who's apparently fingering her in the bike sheds and I will deal with Mark later—for now, my mind is on other things. Lisa asks where I went and I ignore her and Flora continues the conversation. We arrive home in less than fourteen minutes and I can't drive this car anymore.

Oh, do I have to be rid of it...

They won't know this car is linked to the murder, will they?

I am such an amateur. Why didn't I think about these things?

My first kill and it was thrilling and now I have to deal with it. It's like having unprotected sex with a whore—it's great while it happens, but then comes the prodding at your dick and removal of infections.

We arrive home and Lisa and Flora have somehow made up and decided to watch a girly film to which I do not wish to be included. I say that I will pop out and get some snacks for them and Lisa tells me I'm too kind and they enter the house as I enter the garage.

Lisa's car is next to mine. A shitty little Ford Mondeo.

I love this Mercedes.

Why couldn't we have driven her car?

I close the garage door and listen in silence for their movie to start, which it eventually does after what seems like an age.

I open the boot to the Ford.

I open the boot to the Mercedes.

Carluccio is looking at me, leaning his head to the said as if to say *what now?* and I amuse myself with the thought. I take Carluccio out of the boot and he seems even heavier, and I put him in the boot of Lisa's car, the Ford.

That way, if they have a warrant to search the Mercedes...

But they won't.

Of course, they won't.

There is nothing linking me to it.

Or is there?

I get in the Mercedes and I go driving and I go to the supermarket where I pick up crisps and dip and chocolate and all the other things that will make Lisa's fading body more repulsive whilst having little to no effect on Flora's. On the way back I'm at a traffic light and a dickhead cuts me up.

I have my target.

I drive through the red light and speed up and I am alongside him and I look over and he scowls at me and I cut in front of him and speed ahead and in the other guy's anger he rides my bumper. Which is perfect. He is driving recklessly *behind me*. I brake and I brake so hard and so quickly he cannot help but go into the back of me.

My car doesn't swerve in response the collision so I make it swerve in response to the collision and it crashes into a bin and into a lamppost then rebounds into the back of a parked car and he went into the back of me and he was riding my bumper so it will be *his fault*.

The air bag goes off but I'm fine.

I step out to a crowd of people asking if I'm okay, which I am. The ambulance arrives and checks me over and I'm fine and they check the other driver who's fine but is going to the hospital for concussion but we are all fine.

Insurance arrive to take the car and they already tell me they are writing it off. The engine is squashed in on itself, either side is dented inwards, and it is leaking some kind of leak. It is a wreck, barely salvageable.

I give them permission to destroy the car and they will begin the paperwork and they will strip it for parts tomorrow and sell those parts to dozens of other cars in need of those parts and that means *the car will no longer exist.*

Goodbye, Mercedes.

I loved that car, but now I can get another even better, more updated model.

Then I panic.

I forgot something.

How could I be so stupid?

Just as the transporter goes to take off, I shout and I stop them.

I run to the driver's seat and reach over.

I retrieve the crisps and dip and chocolate.

I also take the air freshener. Lisa's car may need it.

Then they leave and I order a taxi, already considering where I will go get my new car tomorrow.

9

_____

THE NEXT DAY I get up and everything is as it was. There are no police at my door and no warrants being issued and nothing on the news about some missing fat restaurant owner and I am fine.

Of course, it's still early, he probably hasn't been reported missing yet, and the investigation will not have begun. Perhaps this was even his day off and him not appearing at work will not be seen as suspicious and I will be given another day. Hell, maybe he was even planning to be on holiday!

I wake up and Lisa is in the bathroom and I walk in as she finishes pissing and I grab her before she washes her hands and I kiss her hard on her furiously dry lips, not caring for the diabolically disgusting morning breath she has somehow acquired.

She says, "Oh, Gerald," and moans and I shouldn't have done that as now she may expect intercourse later—but I am in such a glorious mood that I cannot help but declare it to the world.

Downstairs, Flora is at the dining table eating cereal with

one hand and texting with the other. She barely grunts as I enter and so I stand, and I watch her, and I wait for her to look up.

Lisa is in the living room opening the curtains which gives me a chance to say, in as quiet and husky and rude a voice as I can manage, "How are you, you filthy little trinket?"

She glances up from her phone momentarily to give me that naughty smile she knows makes my body shiver and pine for my dick to enter her wet comfort and enclose it in her heavenly orifice.

Lisa walks in and puts the kettle on.

"You okay, honey?" she asks.

"Yeah," Flora grunts.

"Is that Mark you are texting?"

And my mood drops and I feel irate and when did this Mark become a positive subject for them to engage in? I thought we were hating the wretched little demon?

She glances at me mischievously before she answers, "Yes, it is. We are planning on going to the cinema later."

"Oh, how lovely," Lisa says, as if such a thing should be encouraged.

Then it strikes me that this is Saturday and if Lisa is not otherwise engaged with Flora that means she will insist on spending time with me.

"I'm going to my book club this morning," she says. "Would you mind driving me?"

I am about to groan when I realise I have the perfect excuse.

"I'm afraid I cannot. I was in an unfortunate accident on my way home from the supermarket yesterday and the car was written off. I plan to use today to acquire a new one."

"You were in an accident?"

"That is what I said, yes."

"Why didn't you tell us?"

"I... did not wish to concern you. You both seemed to be enjoying your movie too much."

"And are you all right?"

"I am fine."

"Okay. Glad to hear it. I guess I'll have to drive myself."

She grabs her keys and puts her shoes on.

Flora giggles at something on her phone and so I march up to Lisa and grab her and kiss her passionately with my eyes open and staring at Flora. Two can play at that game.

Unfortunately, Flora is so engrossed in her menial screen she is unable to suffer the jealous effects I was intending.

"Oh, well, I will look forward to seeing you later tonight," Lisa says.

Oh, for fuck's sake. I didn't mean to encourage her.

She says goodbye and leaves and a minute later I hear the revving of a car engine growing faint in the distance.

"So," I say. "This Mark."

"Yeah?" she says, not looking up.

"Put the phone down, Flora, there is a three-dimensional person talking to you."

"Uh huh. In a sec."

I stride up to her and grab her from behind and shove the phone out of her hand and enjoy her yelp as I grab her wrists with one hand and her tiny little breast in the other.

"I said, I am talking to you."

She smiles like she is either enjoying upsetting me or gaining a sexual thrill from my actions, and I am yet to determine which one it is.

"Get on your knees," I tell her.

She acquiesces my request and gets to her knees, looking up at me, purposefully opening her mouth but not approaching my crotch, knowing that this will drive me crazy.

She laughs as she sees the outline of my penis unfurl beneath my corduroys.

"So," I repeat. "This Mark."

"What about him?"

"Who is he?"

"A friend."

"A boyfriend?"

"Could be."

"Does he–"

She unzips me.

She's trying to distract me.

"I said, does he–"

She takes me in her mouth and I feel the warmth of her jaw surround me and there is nothing I could care about in this world right now, not even Mark, not even fucking Mark as she rubs her lips back and forth, flicking her tongue like I taught her. She goes faster and slower and harder and softer at all the right times, cupping my balls and delving the shaft down her outspread tongue and making me convulse and I am already close so close just about to cum as she is delivering me a bout of ecstasy that nothing could interrupt not even *Lisa has driven her car to her book club with Carluccio in the back.*

My penis turns limp and my body stiffens.

FUCK.

I AM

I AM USED.

    I am grateful.

    I am not a child.

    I am the wet dream of a pervert, the epitome of virtue, the dislike of those who know.

    I am not what you think I am.

    You think I want this?

    That I asked Gerald to fuck me?

    That I begged him to take away my innocence, that I pleaded with him to make me think this is all okay?

    Which it is, of course.

    All okay, I mean.

    Because I don't know any better.

    I am too young.

    I was too young then; I am too young now, and I will forever be too young because of what he has done to me. I will never grow beyond sixteen years old, I will forever be left submissive in this state, always finding the world to be as it is now.

    I am not going to lie to you.

    And I am not going to stop him.

But I am not going to pretend that it's something I want, that it's something I wish would continue.

But what would you have me do?

Perhaps you'd say something like I'd tell my mum, or I'd tell him to fuck off, or I would never let him treat me like that.

You wouldn't, you couldn't dare, and you would let him do whatever.

Because I am not you.

But I could be. An ill stroke of fate, a dumb piece of luck, or just to be without the privilege you were so beautifully born into.

I am going to say no.

I am going to stop him.

I am finally going to have the strength I have willed myself to have.

Then again...

I am wrong.

I am never going to have the guts.

I am never going to...

To...

To...

You can picture me, can't you? My head dropping as I write this, sinking, my eyes staring at a floor well-vacuumed, a house well built, a perfect home behind the white picket fence Gerald painted himself.

Do you think I'm crying right now?

Do you think I smile as I write this?

Do you think my hand shakes?

I am not going to be a victim of your sympathy.

Do not pretend that you feel sorry for me. If I was a news item, you'd tut and move on. I'm another statistic you become immune to the more and more you hear about tragic cases such as mine.

Go to hell with your pity.

I don't want your help.

I am easily in control of this situation.
I don't need your intervention.
I am going to do something about it, eventually.
I am fierce. I am a warrior. I am a strong woman.
But, most of all...
I am lying.

10

I IMAGINE that you may ask, should you ever have the chance to engage in conversation with me, why I chose to marry my wife.

Although, if I am honest, it probably wouldn't be the first question you'd ask me, considering I have experienced the delectable ordeal of taking a life. Having known what it is like to attain such a pleasure, I would hypothesise that you would want to know about that.

That aside, it would be a pertinent question to ask me why I married Lisa.

There was a spark when I met her, I suppose. I was briefly attracted to her in the way a child is briefly excited about a new puppy before they realise they have to walk it thrice a day and clean up its shite and watch it pee over the floor as they try to train it.

In truth, I married her because *it is what you are meant to do.*

It's all part of the fancy dress, isn't it?

Society expects me to have a wife, so I acquired one.

Not that I wish to do what society expects me to; rather, I

do this to conform to what society has made you expect me to do, therefore allowing my sick mind—though it is only *sick* as you would refer to it when in company of others who determine anything they can't quite understand as *sick,* therefore removing all the many, many layers there are to human nature in order to keep believing the image you wish to believe—where was I? Ah, yes; therefore allowing my *brilliant* mind to feel I was well hidden.

Marriage is to me what changing colour is to a chameleon. They blend in, unnoticed.

If you were to walk past me in the street, apart from to marvel at the superior quality of my suit compared to yours, you would not look twice. You would see me just as you do everyone else. Which is why, as you may or may not have noticed, I have failed to describe my own appearance in this fruitful memoir. Because you will attach whatever image you think a killer has to these words, whether or not I describe how immensely dull I look. Either way, I look like your friend, or your uncle, or your boss, or, probably, you yourself.

(Though in saying *yourself* I am assuming your gender, something most liberals seem to find as abominable an action as Nazism. If you are a woman, then disregard that *you yourself* bit. Not because a woman can't be a killer. Quite the contrary, you will find many a prison stocked up with murderesses. I simply point this out as I am a man, as you will have most likely assumed.)

So, I sit here, awaiting the return of Lisa. I do not know where the book club is and it would not be a good idea for me to go out searching. I do need to go and acquire a new car, but this will now have to be done this afternoon. I simply have to know whether or not Lisa happened to open her boot to place her bag into it or to see what the umphing noise is every time she drives over a hump. Would she confront me or just go straight to the police station or panic and have some unhelpful witness go do such things for her?

Flora tries to felade me once again, insisting that she should finish what she started. After telling her I am otherwise preoccupied, this being one of the rare times my arousal toward her does not take, she threatens to go suck off Mark what's-his-face instead.

This makes me angry and I consider what I could do to Flora in response, but then I hear a car pull up on the driveway and my entire body tenses.

"Oh, and by the way," Flora says, the front door half open as she readies her quick escape that would not allow me the final word, "Mark has a much juicier cock than yours," and she disappears into the street.

I want to find this Mark and churn him into sausages and force Flora to eat it whilst making her beg me for forgiveness and tell me that he does not taste as nice as me and that his cock is not so great and Lisa has stepped through the door.

She stands there. Frozen. Her arms folded. Looking dumbfounded at me.

"I can't believe you," she says, stone faced and poised, unmoved.

Shit.

I immediately start my plan on what to do with Lisa. I will have to kill her immediately. Could I get that knife from the kitchen draw or maybe I could use something heavy from in here like the television; no that would be rubbish – damn flatscreens – maybe the vinyl player in the corner Lisa insists on having, as if something old fashioned makes her seem more hip, as if worse technology is a fashionable gimmick, and I realise I am distracted and I stand, ready to just do it with my hands, when a smile spreads across her face.

"The air freshener," she says.

Huh?

I feel my head tilt. I am ever so confused. Does she recognise what I am about to do? Is this to throw me off, some clever game she is playing?

"The one you put in my car," she prompts me.

The one I put in–

Ah, yes!

The one I retrieved from the wreckage of my Mercedes before it was towed, the one I put in to disguise the smell of death, that one!

"It just..." She looks like she's about to cry, and Jesus Christ it's a fucking air freshener and she scared the shit out of me. "I know it's small, I know it isn't really much, but such a small gesture, like just getting one and putting it in my car so I get in the next morning to find a lovely smell, it... It's a small gesture that means a lot. It shows you really want to work on this marriage. Doesn't it?"

She's in front of me before I can respond and her arms are wrapped around my neck like she's strangling me, but it's supposed to be affection. She is too small to hug me around my neck, and I wonder why she doesn't just hug my chest instead, and her face turns to within inches of mine and her lips are on mine and that is why. That is why she has insisted on putting her arms around my neck. It's so she can slide her sickly tongue into my mouth and flash it around like a dying eel. It revolts me. She's attractive enough, I guess, she's just not Flora, and she's not a whore.

She goes to take my jacket off and I step out of her embrace.

"I'm afraid I can't," I say.

"Why not?" she says, moving toward me, smiling like I am teasing her.

"I have to go out and get a new car."

"Oh, I'm sure you can spare ten minutes…"

"I really, honestly, cannot."

She freezes. Her face drops. She's angry again, I can tell.

"Are you serious?" she says.

Why would I not be serious? I can't find the punchline if this was a joke.

"Unbelievable," she says, and throws her hands in the air, turns as if to storm out but doesn't. "I think you do something for me out of the goodness of your heart, Flora is out for the afternoon, and we have some time together, and you'd rather shop for a *damn* car than have sex with me. Do you even know how long it's been?"

FYI, dear reader, I assume she meant how long since we last had sex, even though she did not clearly stipulate this.

"Three and a half months. Three and a half months, Gerald! I mean, couples don't go that long even when they are seventy years old."

I sigh. I'd really like to get to that car shop.

I edge toward her.

Her face seems to change.

She gets excited. She thinks I'm changing my mind. She lifts her arms as she goes to caress me.

I take the keys from her hand.

Her face turns to fury.

I leave before the shouting starts.

11

I ACQUIRE MYSELF A NEW MERCEDES. The same model as my old one, except newer, and better. This one has enhanced Bluetooth capabilities, an inbuilt SatNav and cruise control. It makes me wonder why I kept my old one for so long, why I was so hesitant to replace it – maybe it was from some place of sentimentality or fondness, similar to how your supposedly regular members of society might feel toward a sibling or a child or a pet. That car was my pet, and I had to let it go, and now I have a new pet, one that can do so much more.

I spend the rest of Saturday just driving it, pulling up at traffic lights and revving past whatever unfortunate individual is in the inside lane. They can never keep up. Occasionally I roll alongside a BMW, German trash for people who can't drive if you ask me. I've always wondered what BMW stands for, only to conclude from most of the driving I see that it must be an acronym for *Bellend Mong Wanker*.

Before you point it out, I am fully aware that Mercedes is also a German model, but Mercedes at least spent the time developing their automobiles in its Godforsaken country, whilst BMW spent most of their time developing aircraft – or so their Wikipedia pages would assert.

Anyway, it's not so much the car but the people who drive it. Mercedes is for a classy individual. BMWs are for those who suddenly have a little money to buy a car so they buy the shittest expensive car they can afford. They buy with their eyes, not their feel – and a Mercedes feels better; it purrs for its owner, unlike a BMW that just swerves and cuts others up.

I proceed to spend most of my Sunday driving around in this car. When it comes time to refill the gas tank, I do so with a sense of pride, looking around at the other owners to ensure they have at least afforded themselves a wayward glance to admire or envy the car I pour gasoline into.

One young man with a flat cap and tattoos poking out from beneath his vest steps out of a Nissan Almera – a *Nissan Almera!* I didn't even know they still made those. Or, perhaps they don't, and his car is just exceptionally old. Either way I allow myself a silent chuckle at the irony displayed by this stereotype. Society, of course, would expect a heavily tattooed, rough-looking youngster to be driving a car with a loud engine and an invisible sign that says *I have a tiny penis* – the perfect example of a BMW driver, for example.

He looks at me as he returns to his vehicle and I must be staring because he glares at me and mutters something barely decipherable that I just make out as, "What you looking at?"

I chuckle at his impunity, thinking about the image he so poorly feigns. He tries to look tough with his vest and cap and tattoos and attempts at intimidating threats. I feel like showing him what's in my wife's car boot and seeing how he feels then.

The thought suddenly reminds me – *shit!* Lisa's car boot! Carluccio is still in there, and he's bound to start smelling soon.

Just as the thought arrives and I return to my car I see my phone screen light up with Lisa's name. I needn't break any laws by talking with my phone to my ear as my car has Bluetooth, allowing me to patch her through to the speaker of the car, and her voice echoes all around me in some kind of high-technological torture.

"Gerald, are you there?" she snaps, and I think she's annoyed. I have come to recognise this tone, and it normally comes with folded arms, weight on one leg, and a tapping foot. I read a book about body language by a man who claimed to be an FBI profiler, and these were all symptoms he claimed pointed to annoyance.

"I am here," I confirm, enjoying how much this response will wind her up more.

"Gerald, I have barely seen you this weekend, where are you?"

"I am at the petrol station. And now I am leaving. You are talking to me on Bluetooth, how marvellous is that?"

"Great." She doesn't mean it. "Are you planning on coming home at any point?"

Urgh. Home. With that repugnant wife and daughter that is so out of fashion now I have my new car.

"Eventually."

"Eventually? What the hell does that mean, eventually?"

"Eventually. It is an adverb, one that means at some point."

"I know what the fucking word means, Gerald, I want to know what you mean by it?"

I am temporarily flummoxed as I try to understand what exactly she is inquiring. I meant exactly what the word meant, and I don't quite comprehend how I would mean anything else.

"Well," she says, interrupting the silent contemplation. "Just tell me if you are actually coming home today."

I sigh. I suppose I should come home at some point, if only to keep up the pretence of this sham marriage.

Oh, and I do need to sort out that car boot.

"I will be home this evening," I say.

"Right, well I am popping out at six to get petrol for tomorrow, as I have–"

"Wait!" I interrupt, immediately halting her.

A genius idea reaches me that this is, as one may put it, a way to *kill two birds with one stone* (although why you would deny yourself the joy of bashing each bird in separately with its own unique stone I do not know.) I can offer to get the petrol for her, which would also allow me to dispose of the body whilst making it seem like I am doing her a favour, therefore erasing this evident stupor she has worked herself into.

"I will come home now," I announce. "And I will get your petrol for you."

"I need milk as well."

"I will acquire you some milk." Maybe I should get something she hasn't asked for – that's supposed to make people like you. "And some wine."

"Right." She is now poised between annoyance and gratitude. Well, Lisa, which one will it be? "Thank you. I'm glad you've seen the light."

Neither; it is stupidity, then.

I arrive home shortly and park my car with gentle precision outside the driveway. It is now late Sunday afternoon, and no police officers have come to knock on my door, and this reassures me that maybe I did cover my tracks well, or that he is yet to be reported missing, or that I at least have enough time to dispose of the evidence.

After all, it would surely be almost impossible to convict a man of murder without a body.

I wave at Lisa as she scowls at me from the window. I retrieve her car keys and go to her car. I then realise I will need another utensil, such as a hacksaw. I have no such equipment. But I do have a spade and a gardening fork. I also find a duffel bag from a brief period of going to the gym a few years back; a stint that lasted all of three days before I grew tired of the evident-steroid-abusers that barely did any exercise and spent hours just parading around the place in barely visible vests.

I drive Lisa's car until I reach a small village on the outskirts of Gloucester called Birdlip. I come here because I know the police will not. Birdlip is a famous – or infamous, depending on how you look at it – dogging site. The police did, once, have some presence here and convict such offenders, only to find those offenders took their lives due to the shame; a silly thing to do, if you ask me, and another example of society dictating what is normal and what is not normal. If enough people want to partake in public group sex that it has developed its own terminology, that means that it must be normal. Now, as a result, the police stay clear – a *what I don't see I don't have to deal with* kind of attitude.

So I pass a few rocking cars, and keep going far enough past them that they will not try to involve me, and I find a place beneath a tree, surrounded by trees, on an outstretched country road. The angles are such that, should a car drive by, as unlikely as it is down this road; it honestly does lead to nowhere – I know that the car will probably not get a long enough glance to see what I am doing.

I check the coast is clear anyway, which it is, and I take the spade and take the gardening fork and make my way to the boot.

I open it, to find Carluccio staring up at me. His eyes are wide open and he seems shocked that I would be standing over him, but why should he be shocked, did he really think I was going to leave him? His eyebrows are raised and his cheeks are white and his fingers are chubby and gosh he really is an ugly fellow. God knows why I adored him so much. Seems foolish now.

I try to move him and he is stiff. Rigor mortis, it is called. He is also cold. His lips are parted and he is still fat. Even in death, he fails to lose weight.

I do not want to get any blood in the car – not that I think any blood would come out of a body so rigid – so I drag him out of the car and place him on the ground.

I attempt to hack at his neck with the spade. It does little, he is too stiff.

This is going to be tougher than I precedented.

I remove my jacket, something one does when they are about to enter into strenuous physical activity in which perspiration may occur.

I lift the gardening fork and plunge it down to his neck. It takes me a few goes but eventually a few holes are left. I do this at all the joints: the shoulders, the elbows, the waist, the knees, etcetera etcetera.

I then use the spade and thwack down upon these joints I had supposedly weakened, and it takes me a great many strikes to be able to loosen a single joint. I will save you the details, my dear voyeur, about the arduous activity that was so repetitive it would bore you, and that would be a sin I could not forgive myself. I estimate it took upwards of one-hundred-and-three minutes to part many of his limbs from his body, but eventually I managed.

Now to consider what to do with them.

My objective was to put his body parts into smaller body

parts that I could easily dispose of. But how do I now dispose of them?

I could scatter them, perhaps. Place them at various points of the country so that they would be picked up by a fox or a rabid dog or the finder would be unable to place them with the other body parts from so far away.

I could dump them in the ocean, attaching a brick to each limb to ensure it sinks. Then again, that would be a waste of a brick.

Just as I begin to curse myself for not thinking in greater detail about what I was going to do, I see something in the distance.

Animals.

A farm.

And, on this farm, a pen within a field containing many of what I am sure are pigs.

A memory from whence I do not know flutters its way to the forefront of my confusion.

Pigs eat anything.

Anything.

Even bones.

Even clothes.

Even an annoying fat fuck who smells like shit.

Or so I have been led to believe.

Ah, well, time to test the theory.

I take the large duffel bag and shove each of the body parts into it. The bag ends up being exceedingly heavy, but manageable, and I place it in the boot of the car where Carluccio had previously laid intact.

It takes little over sixteen minutes to find my way to the farm. It is an eleven-pound entry fee and another pound to feed the animals. I pay the eleven pounds but neglect to pay the extra pound even though I do, in fact, intend to feed the animals; just not with their bags of nonsense.

I carry the bag through the farm and get a few inconspicuous looks from parents who look away when I meet their gaze. When I reach the pig pen I see them at a troth so full of gunk that I know I could bury the items inside it and they will surely be left unnoticed.

I wait for a family to move on and look around. There is another family approaching but they are still fascinated by the bird section, so I shuffle my way around the fence until I am next to the troth. I open the bag and pour the contents in. I prod down upon a few loose fingers and the tip of a toe until they are completely submerged.

I stand and watch and I learn that pigs *do* eat everything and anything.

"Look, Mum!" shouts the snotty brat of the family just leaving the bird section. "Those pigs are really going at that food!"

"They are, aren't they?" his mother patronises. "They must really be hungry."

I stay until every piece of clothing and every ring finger and every facial figure and every piece of loose scrotal skin is gone. By the time dark has descended, their troths are empty, and I stand there holding an empty duffel bag.

A teenager comes and tells me they are closing the farm soon.

I leave, going to the petrol station and supermarket on the way. When I arrive home, I tell Lisa that there was some kind of trouble at the road leading up the petrol station, more specifically a road accident I fabricated that occurred just as I approached and blocked the road for an unforeseeable amount of time as emergency services intervened.

She believes me.

Flora isn't interested. She's busy on her phone.

She giggles.

"Mark," Lisa mouths to me.

Fuck sake.

I just disposed of one sack of bones.

Ah well, I think I may have an idea for what I shall feed to the pigs next.

12

MONDAY MORNING PROCEEDS just as any other weekday morning does. I wake up next to the same tired wife, eat the same tired breakfast and make the same tired eyes at Flora while her mother's back is turned.

As I sip on my second coffee of the morning, I consider what to do with my day. I could go to the usual café in the morning, out for lunch, and stop at Carluccio's on the way back.

Oh, yes.

I forget.

Although, maybe I should still pop into Carluccio's – if I suddenly stop going now, it would be as if I am aware of Carluccio's absence. Then again, do I really wish to go? I mean, their salmon was good, but the rest of their menu was average at best, and Carluccio's endearing demeanour was the only reason for ever attending.

I will miss that.

Shame.

Flora is texting on her phone again and then I remember – ah, yes. Mark. That was what I was going to do today.

She smiles in a way I've never seen her smile at me and it's not as if it's fair, I suppose, for me to feel any jealousy. Not that I do. After all, I have fucked a great many whores in the time that I have been fucking Flora. I have even reluctantly been consoled into fucking Lisa within that time also, if only to keep up the pretence of love that supposedly exists between us. So how can I be mad when I have fornicated with her mother?

Of course, in another context that would be a lot worse than it is now.

Anyway, it's not jealousy.

I have no feelings toward Flora. She is a good fuck and she makes my dick turn into a rod with the slightest lick of her lips or up-ride of her skirt, but there has never been anything resembling affection toward her, just carnal lust.

So why should I not allow it? Why should I not consent to her engaging in activities with a boy her own age?

Well, two reasons, I suppose.

Firstly, it's irritating. How she buries her head in her phone, how she saves her smiles for his texts, and this constant ignoring of me for the phone when she could be shooting me dirty looks.

Secondly, it's gross. Not the idea of her and this boy's premature penis, necessarily, but I read a while ago that when you kiss someone their saliva can stay in your mouth for up to seven days. That means that if she has kissed this Mark fellow, then she has inadvertently exchanged remnants of his saliva with my own. And it disgusts me to think that I have a pubescent boy's saliva in my mouth. There are many offenders in certain types of penal institutions that may be envious, but I have never now nor will I ever have a predisposition toward young boys.

Please do not see me as homophobic, dear voyeur, that is

not what I intend. I would happily smile at a couple of two men or two women walking past me in the park with their hands and fingers interlocked. All sex is wonderful, whoever is partaking.

It is just that I do not like young boys. It's disgusting and deplorable and those people who do so deserve to be in whatever institution they are incarcerated to.

Flora is my desire, my passion, my obsession. I want to fuck her right now, in fact, and it takes all the restraint I have not to pound her down upon the breakfast table – but, alas, Lisa's presence once again ruins everything.

Was I more attracted to Flora a year or so ago?

With her body less defined and her hips less prominent and her breasts slightly deformed in their early growth than the rounded triangles they have sprung into?

Honestly, I couldn't say.

Because I wasn't fucking her then, and I am fucking her now.

And would like to keep fucking her.

But I do not want Mark's saliva in my mouth, is the point.

And, imagine if you will, she has done more than kiss him. Imagine his penis has been in her mouth. Imagine, even, that he has ejaculated into her saliva.

Would that ejaculate remain for as long as the saliva?

Would that mean that, when she kisses me, she is not just exchanging his pubescent saliva with mine but also his pubescent sperm?

No, this would not do.

And this is why Mark needs to be dealt with.

Not for any possibility of me being a slave to jealousy, but for the grotesque nature of our interactions now that she is exchanging bodily fluids with a man closer to her age.

"Right, I'm off," Flora announces, standing and throwing

her bag over her shoulder without once taking her eyes away from her phone. "I'll be back after school," she says, and glances at me, and it gives me relief that she still gives me the sign that we will later be fornicating; assuming I can do so without losing my erection at the thought of Mark's bodily fluid.

I know I keep coming back to Mark's bodily fluids, and I truly do not mean to, but I just find the whole concept so detestable that the thought keeps re-entering my mind.

"I have PE last period," she says. "I just hope my *teacher* isn't so *rough*."

She glances at me and is that meant to be some kind of code?

Ah, I hate it when a woman does this.

Expects me to read between lines.

I can only understand things at face value, and so I discard the comment and watch her buttocks sway as they mount up the behind of her skirt and she is gone.

"What time are you going to be home tonight?" Lisa asks like she does every day.

"Late," I answer like I do every day.

"It would be good if we could spend some time together."

Oh, this again.

Lisa does this every few weeks.

She gets a sudden wave of sadness that we aren't having a happy enough marriage and she spends a few days coercing me into spending some of my precious time with her.

She does the same thing with diets, gym routines and motherly affection. Feels she is lacking in something, so does an excess of it for days; then the fad passes, and she resumes her life as it previously was.

"Sure," I say, hoping this will suffice.

"I'll see you later on then," she says, and she kisses my

cheek, and I know from this that she is definitely in one of her fads.

She leaves and I check the time.

I best get to school.

I have a student to find.

13

———

WELL AREN'T I A CLICHÉ?

Hovering outside a school in my car like some meandering pervert. I may as well adorn binoculars and an overcoat just to make myself look even more conspicuous.

I try to rethink my tactics. A man alone in a car hovering outside a school during school hours is bound to attract attention, and the last thing I want is someone being able to refer to the strange fellow loitering around. If someone were to see me and be able to recall my car or my appearance following a student's disappearance I would surely be approached by police, perhaps even arrested.

Don't get me wrong, with the lawyers I could afford and just a child's poor description to go on, I would be liberated fairly promptly. But eyes would be on me. All actions on my part would have to cease.

I was reckless with Carluccio. It was a crime of passion, an instinctive attack. I need to be smarter, be more cunning.

I can't expect to be lucky enough to kill the next one in an alley way that has no CCTV trail, or for Lisa to not look in the boot of her car, or for me to rely on the families in the farm being too stupid not to notice the pig was eating a human foot.

No, if I am to continue in my tirade of tampering with nature, to continue to feel the rush and power I felt with my first kill and desperately wish to feel again, I need to be clever.

Because it is a rush.

It makes you feel powerful. Indestructible. Just imagine taking a human life with your bare hands... Your hands, those two paws you hold this book or eReader with – imagine wrapping those fingers around someone's throat or holding a brick up high and slamming it down upon their cranium. Doesn't the thought give you a rush? A high? Maybe even the tiniest of erections (unless you are female, of course, of which there is a higher statistical probability, considering that the majority of people who read books are women between 45-65, in which case, do forgive my presumption of your gender, and hey, fair play to you for sticking with me and not giving the book up for some soppy romance or erotic thriller you can digitally penetrate yourself over once your partner has grown bored with your ever ageing body.)

Where was I?

Oh, yes. The power.

Imagine it.

And don't just read these words and ignore my request, this is not a request, it is a demand. To hell with society's conditioning of what you believe to be right and wrong. You only believe murder is wrong because it has been imprinted on you from a young age. A few hundred years ago and you probably wouldn't survive without a little bit of murder.

So imagine it, really imagine it. The way it feels as their life fades, as their eyes flicker, as they beg you – and they will beg, as you are the one with the power to stop or to continue and decease their breath, halt their heart, end their wretched life.

Doesn't the thought just give you that little surge of excitement?

Well, I can tell you, the thought is nothing compared to the actual experience. I waited so long to actually do it, wanting to feel this power, that I can't believe I deprived myself for so long.

I plan to build up to the big one.

Lisa.

I cannot wait do away with her so I can live the rich bachelor life in my big house with a cook and a cleaner and too many rooms to keep track of!

But, until then, I must build up.

Start small.

With a boy.

A boy of which I am not jealous, I must remind you. It's just an excuse, really. I needed a target and, through Flora, the target presented itself.

Yes, I will kill Mark, maim him, torture him even should the environment give me enough solitude to do so without being caught. Then I will go home and fuck her knowing that I murdered her crush, that I destroyed the only other soul on earth who was willing to place their dirty hands on her filthy, filthy body.

I move my car to the side of the school, where there is a small supermarket opposite, therefore giving me reason to park there that allows me to become less suspicious. From here I can see the bike sheds.

That was where Flora said they had interlocked lips, of course. You may not recall from earlier in the book, and if so, damn your silly memory. Or were you not paying enough attention? Perhaps someone spoke to you at that bit of the novel and you didn't have the guts you needed to tell them to shut up, as you were busy reading.

Well, I assure you, Flora referenced this being the location she took him to.

So, I wait.

The school bell rings on the hour of ten.

And again, on the hour of eleven.

At this school bell, hundreds of disgusting teenagers, most of which are covered in untreated acne or ill-fitting blazers or are wearing skirts that are way too short and way too enticing for their age (not that I actually think they are too short, I quite enjoy it – but society says so, and me asserting it is simply part of my fancy dress I keep frequently referencing.)

Amongst these many young, inexperienced, foolish faces, I do not see my Flora or her Mark. I watch the bike sheds as another couple move to the wooden confines and start to engage in some kind of sordid activity that one may interpret as kissing but would more aptly be referred to as eating each other. Honestly, if one of them was a zombie eating the other I would not be surprised. Their mouths are open wide and are munching and are all teenagers this bad at kissing?

God knows Flora isn't.

The bell goes at twenty past eleven and a group of haggard looking adults usher the children back inside.

I curse my luck for not seeing them, citing break time as the ideal time for Flora and Mark to appear. Just as I consider driving away, something catches my eye, and Flora you little minx, she appears with a boy and she is truanting.

Oh my, you are naughty, aren't you, Flora?

Except, they aren't quite going at it the way the other couple were.

Flora is grabbing hold of his arm and she seems to be dragging him, pulling him as hard as she can to a place behind the bike sheds, where he is reluctant to go. She looks like a ravenous little minx with her top few buttons undone and her tie too loose and her skirt riding up and settling just at the base of her dainty buttocks.

But he is resisting.

This boy, skinny and lanky, with a scruffy, greasy hairdo that would look better placed atop a mop, is resisting this woman who is a far better catch than his. She isn't just out of his league, she's in a whole different sport.

She tries to be seductive, bless her, but she wasn't always that great when not taking direction. She places a hand on the side of his face and tries to lean in and he pushes her off.

He *pushes* her off.

My hand grips the side of the door as I ready myself to burst out and go after the little prick right now, but I remind myself, do not be foolish, do not engage in another crime of passion. I must not get caught.

He says something then storms away and leaves Flora alone.

Flora remains, covering her face, and her body starts convulsing. She seems to be crying. Her whole body is moving with her tears. This isn't just a little cry; it is a full attack of sobs and moans.

She takes out her phone.

Looks at it.

A few seconds later and my phone buzzes.

I check it.

Please be at home after school X X

She puts her phone away and wipes her eyes. She gathers herself, checks herself in the mirror and scoffs at the smudged mascara. She charges away, perhaps to find a toilet.

There is no doubt in my mind now.

Mark needs to die.

Sorry, Flora, but I will not be seeing you after school today. As much as I will miss your precious breasts and quivering lips, there is something I must do on your behalf.

No one rejects my Flora.

And, most of all, no one pushes my Flora.

I drive away and spend the afternoon readying my car boot and my utensils. Weapons that help me kill and help me deal with the body afterwards. I choose things I know will hurt, assured that I will be causing as much pain as I can.

And humiliation.

I want him to feel humiliated, just as Flora did.

I drive around the school a few times, looking for the CCTV cameras. There are only a few on the school buildings, and a few in the nearby streets, but none in the alleyway leading to a football field.

Next to the field are trees with no path leading to a secluded wood.

Not a place people will happen to be walking.

The wood is large and vast, and veers away from any homes. So long as I take him deep enough into it, it is unlikely we will be disturbed.

Unlikely is still not good enough, however – but there are positives in everything; if I am discovered, that just means another person gets to die.

I pop into Carluccio's for the afternoon, just to remove any suspicion. They are all happy and friendly and no one seems to have noticed their boss has not shown up for work. I have the salmon, but it doesn't taste as good when another chef does it.

I return to the field where I wait until 3.15, when school ends.

The masses of students walk past. Bustling as they joke to one another and show off in front of their peers. Some smoke; a disgusting habit, particularly for people so young. A girl walks alone with her head down. A couple passes with their hands intertwined.

Then nothing.

Absence of life proceeds to fill the field for the next few minutes.

Then he appears.

Alone. Away from the crowd.

Friendless.

Probably hung back at school to avoid the bullies that pick on him all the way home.

I'll be doing him a favour.

He doesn't know who I am, which means he isn't looking for me.

He doesn't see me coming as I approach.

He doesn't feel the stub end of the axe as I strike it into the base of his skull.

Or maybe he does, but he is already too unconscious to do anything about it.

I check around me.

I am blissfully alone.

I drag his body into the woods, and I keep dragging until all I can see are trees and I can't hear any cars anymore and I can't see any paths or people and I know that we are totally, completely, unequivocally alone.

14

———

HE COMES AROUND with his head lulling and his eyes flickering and he isn't tied up. He could run if he had the ability. He could even fight me should he feel he had the strength.

But I know this type of boy.

I went to school with this type of boy. They were always called Roger or Phillip or Simon or Keith. I remember one Roger in particular, and he was never hurt in a way that would be obvious to an onlooking teacher – it would always be subtle, such as a quiet name-calling or barging in the corridor and being left out of social activities.

It was all so... tame.

I once stole a frog's eyeball we were dissecting during science class, snuck into his lunch box, and spread it across his egg mayonnaise sandwiches. The teacher searched for ages and kept the class behind, demanding to know where the eyeball had gone, but she never found out.

I had to wait for hours until lunch, sitting alone in the cafeteria, watching, waiting until he took his first bite and gagged. He opened the bread to find a smashed pupil staring up at him, and I chuckled as he threw up in front of all those who so poorly tormented him.

To this day he never knew it was me.

And this boy is so alike to that Roger or Phillip or Simon or Keith. If I were him, I would ready myself for a fight, for a chase, maybe even a barrage of abuse.

But he will do nothing but beg.

Meaninglessly, monotonously, tediously beg.

His eyes look up at me and there's that puppy dog look, that dawn of realisation, that onset of intimidation as he realises his predicament.

After he's done gawking at me, he looks to his right, to his left, and sees how much wood there is and how much room he has for running. He sees that his hands are free, and his legs are moving with liberal ease.

But, just as I foresaw, he does not try to fight, and nor does he try flight.

He tries the third option.

Cowering.

Almost accepting his inevitable fate.

Compromising with himself, a mental monologue that allows him to adjust his expectations until he is comfortable with death, okay with being murdered after an average day at school.

After rejecting my Flora.

"Please…" he whimpers, again, as I expected. "Please… don't hurt me…"

I smile, spreading my grin wide, knowing it will mortify him further. His arms are shaking so hard and if his eyes weren't staring at me so widely I'd think he was having a seizure. In fact, his entire body is convulsing, similarly to how Flora's did when she cried because of him, because of Mark.

Fucking Mark.

"I... I don't know you... I haven't done anything..."

His first instinct is that he's done something to upset me. Such a sad sack of shit, so sure he's warranted this death, that he believes he's done something to prompt me to do this, that he tries to tell me he hasn't.

Imagine having such low self-esteem that you automatically assume you've upset everyone you meet. Given, yes, a man standing over him after taking him captive is a bad example, but still.

"I – I won't tell anyone... I swear..."

No, Mark, of course you won't.

Because a corpse can't talk.

I reach down and he flinches away, his voice quivering with his shudder.

I laugh. I can't help it.

Why doesn't he run?

Why doesn't he fight?

Why does he just get so consumed with fear?

I do forget, of course, that he is just a boy. That he is still, technically, a child. Although now he's a teenager, his teachers will insist he is a young adult which I always thought was nonsense. It's like they have all the responsibility and none of the power – how can you be a young adult when you can't even vote?

Anyway, I digress.

Where was I?

Ah, of course.

Fucking Mark.

"Please, I don't–"

I'm growing tired of his begging now. I reach down and grab the back of his hair. His arms stick close to his body, rigid, tight, but his palms turn upwards, as if his terror is making him retract in on himself, but he wants to show the surrender sign with his hands to show me he means no harm.

Means no harm?

Please.

He's upset Flora. He caused harm.

Not that I actually care all that much – it's just a good excuse.

Now...

How should I do this?

I'd decided not to plan, leaving it to whim. Now I wish I had considered it more. That I had come with some itinerary, or initial starting stages at least, just so I could be mentally prepared.

"I haven't hurt you, I don't know you, please, I'm no one, just let me go, just let me go!"

He's crying now.

And his grey school trousers are soaked around the crotch. It stinks, and it makes me despise him even more.

"Oh, Mark," I say, and tut.

"I'm sorry, I'm so sorry, I'm so so sorry!"

Sorry for pissing your pants?

"I assume it was an involuntary reaction."

He hesitates, no doubt considering what the correct answer is, and he nods.

"Then why are you apologising? Stop apologising."

"Sorry!"

Now he's apologising for apologising and he realises his mistake as soon as he says it. But he can't help himself. Why? Because, as I have pointed out, he is a sad sack of shit who has no self-esteem and needs to get some confidence and *oh my god* I feel that *rage* intensifying, *soaring* through my veins, *consuming* my body, and I am ready.

I am ready.

Oh, I am ready.

I drag him by the hand and he kicks his feet a little bit but still doesn't put up that much of a fight, he doesn't want to upset me of course, to put up a fight would upset me further and the more he upsets me the angrier I get and the more likely I will do what I am going to do and *Jesus Fucking Christ Mark you are a sad sack of shit.*

I retract his head, pulling my arm back, getting a large swing, and I soar his head through the air and collapse his face into the tree trunk.

I hear the satisfying crack of his nose and honestly it gets me a little hard.

I do it again and his face is smeared with blood.

I go into my duffel bag and pull out the axe.

Yes, I think I will use the axe.

I hack on the underside of his knee cap.

I don't want to finish it just yet. I want to relish it.

Carluccio was so quick.

This time, I want to feel it. I want to experience the boy's pain as I inflict it. I want to taste his sweat, feel his blood as it splatters on my skin. My sleeves are rolled up and I put an apron on and I hack away again and again and again and he's screaming and he's screaming and eventually I have to gag him.

We're in the middle of nowhere but I don't think I should push it too much. You could hear that scream a mile away.

Eventually I sever the muscles, but his bone is a little tougher. I have to really put some strength into the swing, into hacking away, into forcing the axe through. He must eat a lot of iron this boy because the bone is strong.

I make a few dents and the muscle is falling away and *shit he's passed out.*

Well, that ruins that.

Play time is over.

No more fun.

Fuck's sake, Mark. I was really hoping to relish this one.

I grow more and more annoyed with him, and it makes it so easy just to slice down upon his neck with the axe.

He still breathes and I haven't got him fully with the first swing. This is to be expected. Contrary to what the movies will tell you, it isn't that easy just to chop into a throat and kill a man. You don't just slice with a knife and expect it to be done. It takes a few goes.

That's why I'm so proud when I get him with the second swing.

He splutters blood and he coughs up some fluid I don't recognise but he isn't breathing anymore.

His eyes open just as the last moments arrive.

I look into them so I get to enjoy it.

I watch that final moment where he realises it's all about to end and there's nothing he can do about it.

I can't quite put into words that expression, you will just have to experience it for yourselves.

And then he's gone.

No more Mark.

No more annoying text messages.

No more irritating giggles.

No more no more no more.

Fucking Mark.

Fucking dead Mark.

Fucking murdered Mark is fucking dead and I did it, and it felt so fucking god damn fucking sodding bloody fucking good.

I take a piece of carpet from the duffel bag and I place it beneath him.

I take out a bin bag that would fit a large dustbin.

I take out a spray.

I use the spray to wipe down the tree.

I gather all the leaves that were beneath him when the blood was splattering and, whether there is blood on them or not, I put them in the bag. This is important, so I spend my time doing this, as I would rather have an excess of leaves than miss any.

I put him in the bag with the leaves, then put the carpet in there with him. It is now covered in his blood, and it was a good idea for me to bring a bit of old carpet to catch it all on.

I drag the bag to my car which I parked off-road just before the trees were too thick. It's a few miles and it takes me a while but I don't mind. I shove him in the boot, and I honestly cannot believe how easy this was.

There was no one around anywhere.

No witnesses.

No one to know.

And I disposed of the evidence – not that they would realise which part of the vast, vast wood he died in, if they realise it was in the wood at all. Maybe the sniffer dogs could find something, but hopefully the elements will take care of any lingering remnants.

I close the boot and I pause.

I breathe in the clean, country air.

I love that air.

Fresh. A hint of manure from a farm somewhere near.

I wonder if that farm has pigs.

Never mind, I will deal with that later.

For now, I am going to enjoy this feeling.

There is no feeling like it.

The power, the rush, the adrenaline.

You really are missing out by trying to fit in with society.

Honestly, if you are not willing to experience this high, then you are the crazy one.

I get into the front of my Mercedes and I blast some music through the Bluetooth. I go for some chaotic jazz by some artist I don't recognise but is somehow on my phone.

In minutes I turn onto an empty country road, and drive into the sunset.

15

I ARRIVE HOME at something past seven, and I can see from Flora's face that she is seething. Her mother doesn't notice, but Flora has gone red and her fingers are gripping her skirt and curling it up and her leg is twitching. I don't particularly recognise when someone else is angry that well – or when they are happy, or sad, or forlorn or giddy or even horny – but with Flora I can always tell all those things. I know her inside and out.

Which is why I knew, before I even saw her, how angry she'd be.

It isn't like it's the first time I've not turned up for one of our little sex sessions. There have been many times my other whims have distracted me, or I've enjoyed a lovely meal so much I've lost track of time or I've frankly found a prostitute that takes my fancy slightly more on that particular day.

But she was rejected today.

By Mark. Fucking Mark.

And I could tell from those tears, from how much she cried when he said no, that it hurt her. That she needed to feel wanted. That, even though she wasn't old enough or mature enough to recognise the subtext to her own mood swings yet – that she needed to be fucked by me, and fucked proper, to get him out of her system. That she needed me to fuck her so she could feel like she was desirable, sexy, and wanted.

And now that she didn't get it...

Her breakdown seems like it's in full swing.

"Oh, Gerald," says Lisa as I walk into the living room. She purses her lip in this way she does when she's about to say something she thinks is important.

"What is it?"

"Flora has not had a good day."

I look at Flora. She looks at me. Something passes between us that Lisa will never know about. Something that she sees but does not understand.

"Mark told her that he doesn't want to be with her," Lisa tells me.

I already knew this.

"Oh no." I pretend to care, feigning concern in a way that's perhaps a little too overdramatic. Still, Lisa believes it. "Why wouldn't he want to be with you?"

"Well, it turns out..." Lisa takes a big, deep breath, looks at Flora as if she's asking for permission, clearly doesn't get it, then turns and tells me anyway. "It turns out Mark is gay."

Mark is what now?

I...

What...

He what...

"She had a conversation with him today," Lisa continues. "They were meant to meet at the bike sheds, which is where they normally meet. And Mark told her. He's gay, and he doesn't think they should be together."

No shit he doesn't think they should be together if he's gay you daft bint.

"Is this true?" I ask Flora, and she nods, and she sobs.

Fucking Mark.

This whole time...

He wasn't rejecting her...

He was coming out!

Shitting fuck sticks.

"I'm sorry to hear that," I tell her, but I can't stop my voice from being monotone.

Hang on.

If I killed Mark, does that make me homophobic?

I mean, I don't think I am. I'm all for gay rights. I always wave at those pride marches when they go past, and I've engaged in sodomy many times – albeit, with women, mostly hookers, some with questionable genders but unquestionable vaginas.

No, it doesn't.

Surely not.

"I was going to go out and get some snacks," says Lisa. "Get a girly movie. Maybe have a glass of wine. Would you stay with Flora while I do that?"

"Sure."

Lisa stands. Kisses me on the cheek.

Flora watches it and hates it.

"Thanks," Lisa says, grabbing her keys.

The front door opens and closes.

Neither me nor Flora say anything until we have heard the car reverse down the driveway and pull away down the street. Even then, we hold each other's stare, hers full of rage, mine full of... well, confusion, I guess. I don't know.

"Is it true?" I ask.

"Where were you?" she asks.

That isn't an answer to my question.

"Is it true?"

"What, that Mark is gay?"

Was gay.

"Yes."

"Yes. It is true. Where were you?"

Fuck.

"Huh?"

"Where were you? You were meant to be here after school. I really needed you."

"I, er... I was busy."

Fucking Mark. Fucking fucking Mark. Fucking stupid Mark.

He was gay.

I killed him because he rejected her, and it turns out he was...

Dammit shit on a brick mother twisted arse hole!

Flora stands. She saunters over to me in this strut she thinks is sexy but only highlights her young age.

"We have five minutes now."

"Huh?"

Five minutes for what?

I killed Mark, and I shouldn't have.

She grabs my dick in one hand and gets a bit of ball in there too. She curls her lip and stares into my eyes. She thinks this is sexy, but in truth, it's quite uncomfortable. And, not to mention, concerning that she can fit my whole dick and ball into her one small hand.

She leans in to kiss me.

"Well?" she says.

I'm still stupefied. Dumbfounded. Mortified.

But I'm still human.

"Eh, fuck it," I say.

Mark is long forgotten.

Well, he isn't, because he's in the boot of my car.

But any reservations I have I quell. He's dead now, doesn't make any difference.

Her lips come closer, almost touching mine, just almost, but as soon as their tender caress meets mine I turn her around and bend her over the table

She doesn't fight it.

I hike her skirt up and her knickers have ponies on.

"I don't want to..." She goes to say something, and I put my hand over her mouth. She bites my finger.

"Please, I need to feel loved, I want to look at you."

Look at me?

I scoff at the joke, pull her knickers to the side, and fuck her quickly over the sink, done and finished so quickly that the floor is wiped and our underwear replaced and we are sat watching cartoons by the end of Lisa's fourteen minute twenty-three second absence, when she returns with a bag of cheesy poofs and some cheap quality wine.

"Miss me?" she says, then looks oddly at Flora. "You look a lot happier!"

I grin.

Flora smiles faintly.

Why wouldn't she be happy? She got what she wanted.

"Well," Flora says, forcing a smile that only I know is forced, "Gerry knows how to cheer me up."

I fucking hate it when she calls me that.

"Well, good on Gerry!" says Lisa as she slides in between us.

And now Lisa is calling me it.

I look at Flora.

There is still something about her that seems dissatisfied, like she didn't get what she wanted.

But I gave her exactly what she wanted.

Lisa starts looking at the films on Netflix and I rest my head on my hand, still able to smell her on my fingers.

16

_____

THE NEXT DAY I get up and Flora has already left.

Lisa quickly gets a coffee to go, asks me when I'll be back, kisses me on the cheek, and leaves.

And I'm left alone.

And this is unusual.

Flora did not say that she would home after school. No implication that she wished to meet me. No sexy eyes over the breakfast table, no teasing me with that skirt, nothing.

I try to understand why, try to replay the previous evening, wondering whether there was something I did that upset her.

But, see, this is the difficult part.

I'm not so good with the human elements of humans. I can never understand why people don't just say that they mean. Everything has to be such an enigma. "Well that was long" never means "that was long" – it means something else. Like it was boring, or too much, or I don't know, I never know, I try to but it's something I just can't decipher.

It's called subtext.

I read about it in that book written by that FBI body language expert. He said that everything is subtext. That every word that comes out of a person's mouth has something attached to it, just as every movement or body stance is influenced by our subconscious.

But I don't have anything attached to anything I say.

I say things as I mean them. I mean things as I say them. I articulate the elephant in the room and I give my observation on it. I never pretend to do anything but.

I decide I will go to Flora's school. I won't go in, and I won't approach, but I will go and watch and see if I can see her and see what kind of mood she's in. If she's crying, maybe it's because of me. If she's saying something, maybe I could try to lipread it and figure out what the *subtext* is.

She will be in lessons until eleven, however, and I will not be able to see her before break time. So I stop at Carluccio's for breakfast, only to find the damn thing is closed.

How is it closed?

What's more, it's closed indefinitely. There is a sign reading *Carluccio's will be closed following a family emergency.*

Well, could my luck get any worse?

I search for somewhere else that does fine dining within the same region, but all I find is a town centre full of vagabonds and the unemployed. After running out of time, I resort to the nearest coffee shop where I get a bacon roll to go only to find that the fat is still attached to the bacon and the roll hasn't even been buttered. I would pull the bacon out and eat it on its own, but I would end up with greasy hands for the rest of the day. That is why we are given knives and forks.

Annoyed at the inconvenience, I return to the school empty-bellied and irritable.

I hear the bell go for break time and I wait and I can see nothing from where I am parked. I decide there will be no harm in getting out, in just walking past the school. Many people walk past the school, it will make no difference if I am seen. I'll just be a passer-by. Another inconspicuous stranger.

So I do, sticking close to the fence, and I can see them all there, in the yard, walking and talking, some playing football, some sitting around chewing gum with open mouths. It is a playpen of morbid potential. So many unpainted canvasses waiting to be covered in shit.

And I see her.

Flora.

On her own.

Her arms are folded. Her body hunched. The book said this is negative body language. Like she is either upset or angry or something along those lines – honestly, it wasn't too specific.

She goes into her bag and takes out a chocolate bar. She unwraps it.

Then she sees something.

Distracted, she walks up to a girl. A girl with pig tails, her body not as developed as Flora's, perhaps a first or second year, who is also on her own. This girl is crying.

Flora offers her the chocolate and she turns it away. Flora seems to insist, eventually placing it beside the girl and lifting her arms in the air as if to say *well I am not going to have it so you may as well.* In the end, this girl takes the chocolate bar and reluctantly eats it, then gives Flora a grateful smile.

"Oh my God," comes the brattish voice of a girl with layers of foundations smacked over her face, standing just outside the school with a cigarette in her hand. If the hideous makeup that she must have awoken in the early hours of the morning to apply did not make her ugly enough, the cigarette did.

"What?" said a girl not quite as ugly, but getting there, wearing almost as much makeup, like a bad imitation of her friend.

"Why is Flora talking to Mark's sister?" the girl asks, every syllable another tone of petulance. "I thought Mark dumped her."

"Haven't you heard?"

"Heard what?"

"Mark didn't come home last night."

The uglier girl drops her cigarette hand to her side and her duck lips stick out like she is feigning concern. It quickly fades away.

"God," she says, though it was said more like *Ggggod-ddddddddddd.*

"What?"

"Mark is such an attention seeker!"

I must move on, otherwise I will have to kill this girl. Not that I imagine the school would be much the worse with her gone – in fact, I imagine there would be a great many students who would no longer be bullied.

As I leave, I keep my eyes on Flora. She talks to this younger girl, engages with her, sits beside her and even puts an arm around her.

She's good, my Flora.

I return to my car and decide I will come home after lunch at the normal time.

Flora will be there.

I'm sure she will.

But what I find when I walk through the door at 3.28 was not what I expected.

17

SHE'S sat at the kitchen with no lights on. Curtains are drawn. The timer of the oven reflects a small, green glow on the back of her head, but that's it.

And she's eating cereal.

In the afternoon.

A massive bowl full of cereal.

I know she knows I'm here as I shut the front door loud enough to announce my presence.

I stand and watch her for a minute.

She doesn't turn around. Doesn't react. Just stares straight ahead, eating cereal, contours of shadows outlining the beauty of her face.

"When is your mother getting back?" I ask her.

She doesn't react. I keep staring, awaiting my answer, and eventually she gives the slightest shrug of the shoulders.

I step toward her, but I don't touch her, nor do I enter her personal space.

Again, this is behaviour I don't understand, and it frustrates me so. Why does she proceed to confuse me?

It is much better when she looks at me with those fuck-me

eyes and freckles on her nose and has already discarded her underwear.

Eventually, she speaks.

"Mark's missing," she says.

"Excuse me?"

"Mark. You know, the guy I was dating."

"Yes, I am fully aware of who Mark is."

"Well done, you."

"He is the gay one."

"Full marks again."

"What of him?"

The spoon pauses halfway to her mouth as she turns and looks at me and I think I see anger, I think I see hurt.

"Did you not listen?"

"To what?"

"I said he's missing."

I already know this.

"Oh no. Do they know who did it?"

"Who did what?"

"... Killed him."

"I didn't say someone killed him, I said he is missing!"

She throws the still half-full bowl into the sink and it clatters so loudly it makes my head throb. She charges toward the stairs, perhaps about to storm up to her room, and I wonder if that's because that's where she wants us to fuck, but then she stops.

She turns slowly, and she looks at me.

I mean, really looks at me.

Like she's picking me apart. Like she's reassembling my pieces and putting the puzzle back together again.

It's a look I've never seen before.

It's a look I do not understand.

And it makes me angry, but I try not to let it.

I don't want to hurt Flora.

I don't.

Not unless I have to.

"Do you even care?" she asks.

"About what?"

"About Mark, for fuck's sake!"

She's shouting now. I'm not sure why, I can hear her fully well, but she's shouting.

"What about him?"

"That he's missing."

"Has it upset you?"

"What do you think?"

"I don't know, that's why I'm asking."

"The guy who dumps me because he's gay goes missing and you ask me if I'm upset? What the hell is wrong with you?"

Oh, a great, great many things, Flora my dear.

"Why is that relevant?" I ask.

"Don't you get it? What if he hurt himself? What if he – he – he went and did something because he was upset, because I reacted like a bitch when he told me?"

Her shouting trails off and she leans against the wall and puts her head in her arms.

She really cares. I can see that.

But I'm not entirely sure what about.

Is it Mark?

Is it me? Have I done something to upset her?

"Did you want me to fuck you slow?" I ask. "Would that make you feel better?"

"Jesus Fucking Christ, is that all you ever think about?"

I don't understand why she's shouting again.

Please stop shouting, Flora.

You're better than that.

And I don't want to hurt you.

"Someone is missing, someone I – I fucking cared about, and it might be because of me, because of how I reacted, and you are just asking how I want to be fucked?"

I look back at her. I know I'm supposed to say something but I'm not sure what.

"You're sick," she tells me, and even though it is in the young person vernacular to refer to something that is good as sick, I do not believe that is what she's doing now.

I step forward and she flinches away, so I step forward again and grab her arms so she can't. I run my hand down her cheek and she bats my arm away, so I hold her tighter, and I lean in and I kiss her.

This is what she wants, isn't it?

What she asked for the last few times?

For something gentler. Something with kissing.

Well that's what I'm giving her, yet she doesn't seem to like it.

In fact, as soon as she bites my lip and I instinctively pull away, I learn that she does not like it.

I taste blood.

She looks up at me, her hair a mess, my hand still on her arms, the rest of her body recoiling away.

Maybe I was wrong.

Maybe she does want to be fucked hard.

"I don't understand," I say. "What is it you want?"

"What is it I want?"

"Yes!"

She glares at me, looks at me so cruelly.

"Not you," she says.

"Excuse me?"

I can't have heard her correctly.

"Not. You."

No, I did.

I know as she enunciated each of those words with clarity and venom.

I understand now.

She's fucking with me.

She's playing hard to get.

"Fine," I say, and I grab her hair, and I go to turn her around and I hike up her skirt but she screams, "No!" and she drags herself out of my reach and runs to the other side of the kitchen and I'm stood looking at her, perplexed.

She's out of breath, but I don't know why as I haven't even done anything to her yet.

She shakes her head.

I look around. It's still so dark.

"It's over," she says.

"What's over?"

She scoffs and looks around as if trying to find an invisible person for affirmation.

"Us," she says. "This. Whatever sordid game we are playing. Whatever it is, it is over."

Wait... what?

She's can't be in a right mind.

This whole Mark thing has messed with her head.

Maybe she just needs to lie down.

Or maybe she just needs to feel me inside of her again.

I know she'll want me if she feels me inside of her.

I go to move toward her, but she shifts so the kitchen side remains between us.

"Flora, what are you doing?" I ask.

"I'm keeping away from you."

"Why?"

"Because you are sick and demented, and if you come

near me, I will scream, and I swear, I will tell my mum about this."

Woah.

You'll what?

I feel my lip curl and I try to stay calm.

I really, really do not want to kill Flora.

But I can already feel my predisposition leaning that way. I can already feel her fate changing, the course of her life shifting to one where she ceases to exist and I feel a sharp pang of regret as I stand over her lifeless body.

"I should have ended this long ago," she says. "All you do is use me. You never loved me. You never loved me like I loved you."

"Love?" I echo, and I am astonished.

She thinks she loves me?

She thinks this is love?

My dear, I do not know what love is.

I have not felt it, nor have I seen it or tasted it or heard it. As far as I know, it does not exist.

She has a far more twisted mind than I ever thought she had; she must do to think up something as wicked as love.

"You..." She's crying now. I hate it when she cries. "You... you never loved me. Did you?"

Is this a surprise to her?

Is she actually needing me to verbally confirm this?

"Did you!" she screams so hard her voice breaks.

"No..." I say, my voice hushed. "And I never expected you to love me."

She is shaking her head more and more vigorously, crying more and more vigorously. Everything about her reeks of a breakdown, and I need to be careful, need to be wary.

She is clearly unstable, and she could be more dangerous than I realise.

"You don't even love my mum, either. Do you?"

"... No."

"And you never have."

"... Of course not."

She shakes her head as if this is some profound enlightenment.

"Then leave," she says. "Leave us both. You're not my real dad, you don't owe me anything, you don't owe her anything. If you don't love either of us, then why stay? Why put us through this?"

"I have to."

"Why?"

"You wouldn't understand."

"Then try me."

Try her?

Should I even try to verbalise my reasons?

Would she even begin to understand?

"Because it looks normal," I say. "Because it makes me fit in."

"What?"

"Because it's part of my fancy dress, Flora. People have wives so I have a wife. People have stepdaughters, so I have a stepdaughter. It's all part of the image."

"You have invaded my family for *image*? What kind of monster are you?"

This rings many, many alarm bells. Not just one, but many, screeching and wailing, setting off terrors in my mind.

She thinks I'm a *monster*.

She thinks like *you*.

Like *society* has taught her to.

And now she can see through it.

But I don't need to kill her.

Not if I can get inside of her.

She believes it when I'm inside of her. She knows what this is, what it amounts to, what role she plays. She knows the passion she sparks in me and the passion I spark in her, and she's forgotten it, but she'll remember it, I know she will – but only when I'm *inside* of her.

"Come here," I tell her.

"No."

I step forward and she moves so the kitchen side still remains between us, and this is getting frustrating.

"Come here," I tell her.

"Come near me and I'll scream!"

I know you will, you little minx, and this is how I know I'm right. Because I always make her scream, and she wants me to make her scream again.

"I said come here."

"Stay away!"

I dive across the kitchen side and she yelps and she runs and I run after her and I'm faster than her so I catch her, and I wrap my arms around her, and I laugh as she cries out, "No, no, no!"

But it's part of the game we play.

I turn her around and I force my lips on hers and she tries to bite again but I bite back and two can play at that game.

I turn her around and she struggles but I grab her hair and hold her head down on the dining table.

Finally, she submits. She cries but there is no more struggling, no more fighting.

It's just us.

And I know she'll feel it, I know she will, as I lift up her skirt and drop her knickers and I'm already hard, already ready, and I slide myself in and *my God* I could never live without this. She is just so warm, so tight.

I lean over her and I speak in her ear as I thrust, and she cries with every thrust, just like I know she will.

"I told you you'd feel it," I tell her. "I told you you'd feel it."

And I'm close and I'm getting faster and I'm closer and that is why.

Why I don't hear the car.

Why I don't hear the front door.

Why I don't hear the drop of a bag from the doting mother who had come home early to surprise her daughter.

In fact, I don't even realise Lisa is there until she screams out, *"What the fuck are you doing to my daughter!"*

18

———

MONOGAMY IS one of the most bizarre of society's concepts. I don't think it comes out of necessity or reality, but rather out of jealousy that under-hands all human interaction motivated by this word *love*.

And let's look at *love* for a moment.

So many people say they love someone else, and that's fine, and each time it means something different from the person who says it.

So say you love someone, you dote your life to them, and perhaps you mean it, and perhaps you even stick with it, and don't become one of the exceedingly high statistic of marriages that end in divorce. You live together until you die.

You might then say to me – *well I've proved love exists.*

To you, I would say, well, hang on – I reckon – no, in fact, I guarantee – that the person you die with was not the first, or the only, person with whom you claimed you love. Even if you were fourteen in an early romance, or a fleeting infatuation in your twenties where you finish it and meet this next person and declare that you weren't previously in love because it doesn't compare to what you have now.

That's irrelevant. You still said you love them at the time.

And this brings me back to what I asserted a moment ago – *love* is just a word. A word that springs jealousy. And it is jealousy that forces monogamy, not common sense.

And, for fuck's sake, your wife or husband or girlfriend or boyfriend or partner or whatever is not listening right now – you have to force monogamy, don't you?

Maybe it's easier on some days, when things are really good. But throughout an entire life with someone, you would undoubtedly be lying if you were to claim you weren't ever in the least bit tempted.

Because we are cavemen and cavewomen.

We fuck and we reproduce as nature intended, and nature never intended for us to fuck or reproduce with just the one partner.

And we don't. Rarely do you come across someone who only has sex with one person for their entire lives – and, if you do, despite what that person says, I do not believe their singular sexual history was by their own choice.

Unless it was because they were abstinent for God.

God, which is the only thing more ridiculous than monogamy.

I digress.

My point is, I just fail to see why Lisa is so immensely incensed.

Albeit, her daughter won't be seen as the optimum choice for my indiscretions. And, from the perspective she had as she entered the room, I'm fairly sure she assumed I was attacking Flora, that I was forcing myself upon her.

But seriously, did she expect me never to search for something else? It is in our instinct to search out new sexual conquests, and the only thing more ridiculous than denying that is refusing to go along with it.

Flora utilised my immediate shock to rush out of my reach and push her skirt back down.

"Don't do that," I tell her.

"What?" she groans, almost indistinguishably from the amount of sobbing she is doing.

"Pretend you weren't party to this."

"I wasn't!"

"You like it when I'm rough, when I bend you over and make you–"

"I don't! I don't like it! You don't listen to me, I said no!"

"And I told you you'd feel it when I was inside of you."

"What the hell is wrong with you?" Lisa snaps. She is moving toward her daughter and I am not going to let them form some fake united front against me, so I step between them, and Lisa freezes.

But she doesn't back down.

I can see the wrath of a woman scorned, the fury of a protective mother. This, again, is nature. Protect your young.

It's the first time I can see something real about her.

"Get the *fuck* out of my way," she demands. "I wish to get to my daughter!"

I look at Flora.

Tearful Flora.

Distraught Flora.

Fake Flora.

"No," I say, my voice calm and deep and grave. One of us has to keep some rationality in this situation.

"I said get out of my way," she repeats, as if this confident vigour, this instinct to protect, is going to do anything to deter where I'm standing.

I even chuckle a little, amused at the situation.

"Why don't you make me, Lisa?"

"Mum..." Flora whimpers.

"Cut it out!" I snap, and now I am getting angry. "Stop pretending! Stop making it seem like you didn't want it!"

"I didn't want it! I never wanted it!"

"You mean," Lisa says, edging toward me, "this isn't the first time you've attacked her?"

"I have not attacked her."

She tries edging forward again.

"Honestly, Lisa, if you come any closer, I will be forced to kill you."

"Mum..."

Lisa knows she won't get past me, and inevitably her next instinct is to arm herself, so she sprints to the kitchen where she takes the sharpest knife from the knife rack and holds it out to me like it's a present she won't let go of.

I grin.

I can't help it.

"What are you going to do?"

"I'm warning you."

"Are you going to stab me, Lisa?"

"Get out of my way."

"But I'm your husband."

"I'm going to call the police."

This stumps me.

The police.

That's the last thing I need.

I can't risk them discovering...

Oh, Lisa.

Why did you have to say this?

Why did you have to go and ruin a perfectly good sham of a marriage?

Why have you forced me to have to kill you?

"Mum..."

"Just stay there," Lisa says.

I walk toward my wife.

I walk toward her and she backs away at first, then stays strong, holding the knife toward me.

"Don't come any closer!" she says.

I can't stab her, it's too messy. But I don't have anything else.

Ah, well.

Flora is here.

Two hands will get this cleaned up twice as fast.

I walk until I'm a step away and she holds the knife out and she looks at her daughter for what will probably be the last time.

"Give me the knife," I tell her.

"Get out of my house."

"Give me the knife, or I will have to take it from you."

She makes her final mistake. She swipes the knife toward me, I grab her wrist and, whilst I'm not the most muscular or well-built chap, I am far stronger than she is, strong enough to twist that knife around and push it toward her with her own hands.

She releases it and it drops to the floor.

Good idea. Now I don't have to be so messy.

I grab the back of her head, getting a good tuft of her hair, and she yelps, and if she thinks this is pain then she is not going to cope well with what comes next.

I bring her head down into the marble of the kitchen side so quickly and with such force, with everything I have in fact, that her nose clicks out of place and a few teeth clatter into the sink.

This gives me an idea.

I put the plug in the sink and pour both the taps. I make it as hot as I can just to make it worse for her.

She groans, groggy, and I smash her head against the side

again. I pull her head back and her eye is black and it won't open.

Once the sink is full, I push her head into it and hold it there. The heat of the water is harsh on my skin and I have to endure it even though it's tough.

Her arms push a little bit, but she's already pretty out of it and losing consciousness so it's not like they do much.

It doesn't take long for her body to fall limp.

But I know this is not the end. I know your body falls unconscious before it dies.

So I hold it longer, probably longer than I have to. I hold it there and wait, and three minutes go by on the oven clock, and I see Flora watching me out of the corner of my eye.

She doesn't move.

She stares at me.

The fact that she doesn't run can either be one of two things.

A sign of her adoration for me and the fact that she would forgive me for killing her mother, for us.

Or that she is so shocked her legs have become dead weights and she is completely unable to move.

I pray it's the first, but I can't take any risks.

I decide it's been long enough, and I let go of her mother's head, and her body just stays there, limp and heavy.

I reach beneath her head in the sink and take out the plug.

When the water has drained, I see her eyes are closed, so I open them.

Her pupils have fallen to where gravity has pushed them – though I can only see one clearly, of course, as one of her eyes is still mangled.

I look at Flora, who looks at me, her mouth *catching flies* as the saying goes.

I don't really like sayings, but I do like that one.

"Get the cloth," I tell her. "We need to clean this up."

We'll clean it up and then we'll go.

We can't stay here.

Not anymore.

But that's okay, because when we get in the car and we drive, the car has Bluetooth.

I have the perfect playlist that Flora will love.

19

———

FLORA DOES FAIRLY WELL, considering.

I mean, I'm fine.

But Flora still suffers some predisposition toward the human condition, and this means that I should expect her to feel some sadness toward her mother's demise.

It is said that there are five stages of grief – denial, anger, bargaining, depression, acceptance. I know this because I often go through these five stages when I realise it's time for me to go home to Lisa's tea.

Denial – *it can't be real, I am not going home for Lisa's tea.*

Anger – *why do I have to fucking bother, this is so shit.*

Bargaining – *ah, well, it's just something I have to cope with to keep up the façade.*

Depression – *I really wish I didn't have to though, this is shit.*

Acceptance – *well, I best get going.*

Luckily, I will no longer have to go through those five stages.

Flora doesn't appear to have entered these stages yet, however, and I am hoping that's because she doesn't need to. She is still yet to say anything, and she is walking around most peculiarly. It is like every step she takes is on a floor of squeaky toys and she is trying not to wake a baby. Her movement is so stiff and cold, and her face is so pale and empty.

It will pass, I'm sure of it.

Either way, she does everything I say, as I say it. I hope this is out of understanding and adoration rather than fear or dread, but I am yet to see any evidence either way.

She has sprayed the kitchen side as thoroughly as I have requested, using the best quality antibacterial spray we have. You can't just spray it a little, you have to coat the surface, wipe away, then repeat again and again until you are sure that any smidgen of blood, however invisible, is gone.

She does struggle, however, when I tell her to help me lift the body.

She stares at it, then rushes to the other sink where she throws up.

Which is annoying, as it delays us further, and she has to spray the sink multiple times as well.

I let her off, and I drag the body, even though it feels so much heavier than it did when she was alive. Flora opens the doors for me at my request until we make it into the garage via the door of the house.

She opens the car boot of Lisa's crappy car, and I shove Lisa in there. I close the boot and I look at Flora.

She doesn't look back at me.

"I need to know," I say, "whether you are going to be a burden or not."

She still doesn't look at me.

"Flora, you are being rude."

Still.

I lean forward, move her chin with my thumb, and try to lift her face but she snatches her head out of my reach.

I forget she is just sixteen. She is young, and as filthy and adult-like as she is with her sexual maturity, maybe she has not built the resilience to know how to remain polite in such situations.

So I grab her chin with my whole hand and grip hold so she can't wriggle out of it. I lift her head until it is directed toward me, yet she still doesn't look at me.

"I really don't want to kill you, Flora," I tell her. "I need you to look at me."

That worked.

She looks at me, but it feels like a scowl, or a look of caution, which is not what I wanted. I want her to feel at ease with me, to know that this is good, that it means we can do whatever we want.

We are free of secrecy.

Free of the burden of an overbearing wife and mother.

No more stupid girly nights as a solution to her problems.

We will fuck all of her problems out.

Do it the real way.

But for now, I need to be clear. I need to shock her into acquiescing to my requests. I cannot deal with any unpredictability.

"This can go one of two ways, Flora," I tell her. "Either we are happy. We deal with this and ride off into the sunset. You cooperate and do as I say and we get out of this safely and nothing needs to happen that I will regret."

I take a moment to let the first option sink in, then I continue.

"Or I will kill you. If you run, I will catch you. If you freak out, I will catch you. I know you dote upon me and do not wish to upset me, but at the moment you are acting really odd. So, do as I say, and I won't have to do with you as I did with your mother. Understand?"

She doesn't move.

"Nod for me, Flora."

She nods.

Her face seems to have changed from a glare to that of dread. I can't understand expressions very well, but I can feel her body shaking, I can see the wide-eyed sting of fear in her eyes.

That's fine. She needs to be scared at the moment.

"Get in the car."

This is the first test.

I get into the driver's seat.

She could easily run back into the house, or she could push open the garage door. She could make an attempt to get away from me before I get out of the car.

But she doesn't.

She heeds my warning, and she gets into the passenger seat.

"Good girl," I say, and I pat her leg, and it's still bare and I can still feel her skin in my palm and it angers me when she flinches away.

I remind myself that her behaviour can be erratic. It will pass.

I drive and we remain in silence. One of the first times I haven't had to hear her yattering in my ear, and I enjoy the peace. Maybe she is trying, after all.

After an hour of driving we make it to the lake.

This is where Lisa's suicide will take place.

A death by drowning.

We are surrounded by woodland and there will be no camera to pick us up as we walk our way to the nearest taxi rank.

We have left our phones at home, quite intentionally.

"Get out," I say, and Flora does as I tell her.

I move to the boot and open it.

Lisa looks at me. That same judgemental, incessant stare.

I want a memento.

Something to remember each kill.

I take her wedding ring and place it inside my pocket. I then drag her to the ground and pull her to the driver's seat and prop her up.

It's dark now and there's no one around. I check multiple times for prying eyes, but we are safe.

"Come here."

Flora does as I say.

I put my hands on the back of the car and begin to push. I indicate for her to join me. She does nothing.

"Flora," I prompt her.

She still does nothing.

She stares at the car, away from me, and there are tears in her eyes.

Gosh, I forget – this is the first time she's disposed of a body. She must be worried it won't work, that we'll get discovered.

Maybe I should be more understanding.

I move toward her and I put my arms around her.

She does not reciprocate, but that's okay. I just hold her for a moment, pressing her head against my chest.

I kiss her forehead.

She still doesn't look at me. If anything, she's crying more.

We don't have time for this.

We can deal with it later.

"Whatever is going on, save it," I tell her, more assertive and less sympathetic. "Deal with it later. Right now, I need you to push the car."

I move to the back of the car and get ready. She still doesn't join me.

"Flora, I don't want to hurt you."

This seems to work, as she reluctantly takes her place. We both push – not that I notice a difference, but she is young and small and weak, so it's not surprising.

The car rolls quicker and quicker, gathering speed.

"Let go," I say, and the car plummets forward, and sails off the end across the small pier with a splash.

It is submerged within seconds.

And she is gone.

Lisa is gone.

I am free.

Liberated.

Void of my figurative shackles.

I lift my head to the sky and feel a drop of rain. I relish it. I take a big breath in, hold it, and release.

I can't help but smile. I even laugh a little.

I feel giddy.

I am free.

Flora watches me, but she doesn't join in.

She will eventually. Just give her time.

I finish my celebration and I look at her, wondering when I will see her smile again.

"You did well," I tell her. "I'm proud of you."

She cries harder now. It's most perturbing.

"Please," she says beneath the sobs. "Please, just let me go. I won't tell anyone."

Well this is unexpected.

Firstly, that she would wish to be let go. I thought she was obsessed with me.

Secondly, that she wouldn't tell anyone. Of course she would. If she doesn't wish to be with me, she would inevitably be on her mother's side and want her killer caught.

I get angry but I quell it.

Now's not the time.

I grab her hand. She tries to pull free, but I grab harder because dammit we can finally hold hands and we are going to do so.

"I did this for us, Flora," I tell her. "I did this for us."

I guide her through the woods, and it's almost midnight by the time we emerge, wet from sweat and rain. We find a taxi who returns us to our home.

Our sweet, empty home.

Where we can share it together without interference.

Alone.

Where we can fuck *all day long.*

WEAKNESS IS

Weakness is saying no and doing it anyway.

Weakness is submitting when you refuse to submit.

Weakness is as weakness does because weakness is...

Who cares?

Who really cares?

You're not reading this to hear the lament of the victim. You're reading this for the entertainment of the perpetrator's violent descriptions.

The blurb did not tell you you'd have to read my useless diatribe, did it?

Skip it.

Go ahead, swipe the Kindle or turn the page or do whatever you must to avoid my useless ramblings.

Weakness is going on and on about your misfortune and doing nothing about it.

He said he did it for us.

For us.

Weakness is being responsible for your mother's death.

Weakness is forcing yourself to be numb so you can survive, so you can endure, so you can try to make some kind of effort to see it through until...

Until...

Until weakness is no longer all I am.

Weakness is this constant moaning and whining and going on and on about oh how bad my life is how bad everything is how bad how awful and I hate it because I AM SO FUCKING WEAK.

Why did I have to be this way?

Why did I have to be the person who moans about my supreme weakness in never doing anything that matters about anything that affects me?

I am too young to be strong.

Strength is something my mother should have taught me.

Weakness is all she has left behind.

20

I KNOW that if Flora is to live, I must trust her.

But, given her unsettling reaction this evening, you can understand why it may be tough for me to do so.

I decide to be kind, to try the nice tactic, to try to provide to her the warming sensibilities her inept mother seemed to be so successful with.

I run the tap to ensure it is cold, then fill a glass. I transport this glass into the living room where Flora sits.

She looks empty. Like she has deflated against the cushion. Her wrists point upwards and her eyes stare at something in the lower corner of the room, but when I look there's nothing there, and I can't understand what she is doing.

"I brought you some water," I tell her.

She says nothing.

I reach the glass out to her, but she doesn't take it.

She doesn't even move.

She remains, statically immobile. If it weren't for the faint rising of her chest, I would wonder whether she was dead.

"Flora, I brought you something."

Nothing.

"Flora, I have done you a favour."

Still nothing.

"Flora?"

She ignores me.

I launch the glass across the room and it smashes against the wall which makes her body flinch and damn, finally, we have a reaction.

"I'm sorry," I say, clenching my fist, trying to contain the anger. "I just really dislike it when someone ignores me."

She turns her eyes to me and she has the same stink-eye as her mother. It's a glare, and I can see it's a glare, I may not be able to understand much, but that I can be sure of.

I take to my knees and waddle toward her, taking her hand in mine, but she pulls it away and pushes herself further against the seat, further away from me.

"You can move your stuff into my room," I tell her. "Would that make you happier?"

It doesn't.

Maybe I'm rushing this.

"Fine, I won't force anything, not quite yet. It's been a busy night, and we both have things to think about."

She still looks at me that way.

"Flora, if you do not talk to me then I feel it will be necessary for me to become violent."

"What do you want me to say?" she says, and her voice is low, husky, venomous.

"Well, I need to know I can trust you. I need to know that, should I let you go to school tomorrow, you will not say anything."

She doesn't answer me.

"Flora, really, it is essential that you remove my doubts. I don't want to be forced to kill you."

"Forced to kill me?"

"No, that's not what I, I mean, Flora..."

I drop my head and shake it, but only for a moment, then I pick my head up and look at her and she is really taking some patience today.

"I need to know I can trust you. I need to know that, the minute you're at school, you aren't going to go babbling to someone."

She goes to answer, but she doesn't.

"I need to hear you say it, Flora. I need to hear it from your lips. Repeat what I say – I am not going to tell anyone."

She doesn't say anything and I am forced to put my hand around her throat and squeeze just enough to temporarily cut off her breath.

"Say it," I instruct her. "I am not going to tell anyone."

"I am not going to tell anyone," she replies, and boy what a little threat does to get you talking.

But it's not enough. I still don't trust her.

Not yet, anyway.

Not enough.

"I want us to be happy, Flora. Really, I do. But I am prepared to do what I have to in order to protect my innocence. So, know this – if you say anything to anyone..."

I lock eyes with her and I turn deadly serious.

"You saw what I did to your mother, didn't you?"

Her eyes widen and I can see true fear in them – now that is an emotion I do know.

"*Answer me!*" I bellow, impressed by the power of my own voice.

She nods vigorously.

"I made her death quick, didn't I?"

She hesitates, then nods.

"That was kind of me wasn't it?"

Another hesitation, and she nods. She does so not

because she agrees, but because I am accessing her terror, and that is what I need.

"Your death will not be quick, will it?"

She stares at me then shakes her head.

"I will hack you up into pieces and make you watch until the very last moment that I snatch your life away. You can go to the police station and they can try to protect you, but I will find you whether now or in twenty years or however long it takes. You will always be looking over your shoulder, won't you?"

She nods.

"And if you even mention or hint at anything I will be there to end everything. Won't I?"

She nods.

"I will take that metal bed frame and ram it up you until it comes out of your mouth, won't I?"

She nods, now with tears in her eyes.

"I will shatter the window into tiny shards of glass and make you eat them until the inside of your throat bleeds, then make you eat them some more, won't I?"

She nods. Tears are dribbling down her cheeks, her vision is obscured by them. They are cascading and running and bombarding her shoulders with their salty taste.

"I will cut your breasts off and force feed them to you, and you will eat them, and taste them, won't you?"

Another desperate bout of sobbing as she nods.

She understands.

She won't do anything.

And now is the time to be a good stepdad.

I pull her in close, holding her to my chest, and I let her cry.

"Now don't ever make me say those things again, all right? I do not want to hurt you. We can be happy, can't we?"

She nods but I want to hear her say it.

"Can't we? Tell me."

"Yes, we can."

And that answer is like a sweet symphony. It is a delight to my ears, ecstasy through her fragile voice.

"Now kiss me," I tell her.

She lifts her head to mine and I don't wait.

Her lips are wet from those tears and I can taste her running mascara.

We won't have sex tonight.

There is too much to take in, too much to consider.

But I keep her close. I sit next to her and hold her to me as I put the television on.

She convulses with tears every now and then, sometimes she shakes with what I presume is fear, and sometimes she just stays completely stiff.

Either way, I do not let her go until it's time to say good night, at which point I take her phone and send her off to the warm protection of her duvet.

21

WHEN I AWAKE, the birds seem to be singing a more tuneful song, and the sun seems to be shining just that little bit lighter. My bedsheets smell fresh in a way they never have in the morning, and the bed feels big; so big I can stick out my arms and wave them like I was making a snow angel and there would be no one there to moan and bitch at me.

I wake up and I use the bathroom and I don't wipe the rim afterwards.

My towel is alone on the drying rack and it is dry, actually dry, and do you know how long it's been since I've had a dry towel?

Normally it would be two towels shoved onto the same rack all scrunched up because they don't both fit and *it's only fair that we share* yet now, now, right now – the towel has spread out across the rack and is crispy in a way that will dry my body so sufficiently when I come to use it.

And it dawns on me... I can buy a new house.

I have the money to go out today and pay cash for as big a house as I want.

And I could do all kinds of things to that house. It could

be set up with rooms I will never use and would take officers ages to search and you would get lost in and, oh my I just had the best idea – it could have *shutters*.

So, if there were an intruder, or an unwelcome guest, or someone who has run loose of my captive, a flick of a switch or the push of a button and shutters could fall down around the outside and they would regret the moment they fell prey to me.

I can stop wearing mediocre suits and start wearing fantastic suits. I could go today, in fact, to the tailor and get a whole new rack of them.

I am filthy fucking rich and it doesn't matter who knows it.

I hear Flora downstairs. She is up. The crispy rattles of a cereal box tell me that routine has been restored.

There is still one task I need to perform, something I need to achieve before I can remove all suspicion from me.

I pick up the phone and dial 101. The non-emergency line.

It rings and I get ready. I jump up and down a little bit, make myself out of breath, and ready my performance.

Right, here goes.

"Hi? Hi! Yes, I didn't know whether to ring you or 999, I don't know, is this the right one? It's just, I'm so scared, but... Yes, it is my wife... My wife, she didn't come home last night... No, it is not like her, not like her at all, she is always home in time for dinner and me and her daughter are so worried, it's just not like her... Yesterday, when she left after breakfast... Yes, thank you, thank you so much."

They say they will send the police around right away.

Marvellous.

I leave the pleasure of my bedroom for the delight of the hallway. Soon, I will have a huge bedroom and a huge hallway and multiple sets of stairs, all with fantastic architecture.

For now, I make my way down the delectably small set of stairs and mosey into the kitchen.

And there she is.

Like a ray of warm light, sat at the kitchen side, a bowl of cereal before her. She doesn't smile as she greets me, but she doesn't flinch or sneer either, so I guess that's progress. She doesn't look at me and her spoon hovers in the cereal that she doesn't eat.

But nothing can ruin my mood.

Not even this irritably sullen performance.

"Good morning," I say, and place two pieces of bread in the toaster. Normally I don't like toast, but today, I am feeling like a spot of jam.

She doesn't reply, so I lean on the side and look at her expectantly, and eventually, I get a marvellously insincere, "Good morning."

"How are we today?"

She looks in my direction but does not look at me.

"I've been better," she says, still so grumpy.

She misses her mum. That's it, surely. Maybe I underestimated their bond. I always supposed that if she was willing to fornicate multiple times with her mother's husband then she can't particularly care that much for her. But, as we have already established, my understanding of human behaviour is quite limited, and Flora is a complicated person at best.

My toast pops and I place it on a plate. It's a little too burnt, but that's fine, it'll do. I spread some jam on it and the jam is supermarket own brand and I cannot wait until I replace and restock every item of food in here.

"I have a secret," I tell her.

She lifts her eyes in my direction again, but still doesn't look at me.

"I am rich."

She scoffs.

"I am being serious. I always hid it from your mother as I didn't want her to have the money, but I inherited more than ten hugely successful businesses from my father, and I have so much money that we need never make ourselves food again. We can eat out, or, even better, hire a chef. We can get a bigger house, you can have your own quarter, it will be... magnificent."

She doesn't believe me. I can tell.

I suppose that's inevitable. It's got to be quite a shock.

"One more thing," I say. "The police will be here shortly."

Now she looks at me.

Now she drops her spoon and meets my eyes.

"Are you turning yourself in?" she says, and I'm not sure if I detect a modicum of hope in her question.

"Gosh, no," I say. "I am going to report a missing person. That way no suspicion will be on us."

I am careful to say *us*, instead of *me*. After all, she aided and abetted. She helped me transport the body, she helped me be rid of it, and she has said nothing. She is now more than just an accomplice. She is part of the murder.

And I hope she knows this.

"I need to you to pretend like you are sad," I tell her.

"I *am* sad," she says through gritted teeth. I feel like there're things she wants to say and she's either too fearful or too embarrassed.

"What are you so sad about?"

Her jaw drops and she doesn't answer.

She starts crying again.

For fuck's sake.

I can't deal with this anymore. I wave my hands in the air.

Then I think – is this acting for the police? Is she getting ready?

If so, wonderful.

If not...

I don't have time to ask as there is a knock on the door. That was mighty quick!

I open it and welcome the police in. My performance has resumed and I imitate how I see people act. There is a twitch in my eye, I fold my arms, retracting my body language. I hunch my posture and I shorten my strides. I am devastated, as far as they are concerned anyway, and that is the most important thing.

They see Flora crying and I watch her, looking for any looks she gives them or messages she tries to pass. To her credit, she does not. Maybe I can trust her.

We go through the routine of the situation. When I last saw her, whether she's done anything like this before, whether I've tried calling her, and so on and so forth.

They say that they will begin their search and put out a description, and that will get things started, and they will be back in contact soon.

Then, just as they go to leave, Flora ever-so unexpectedly says something.

"Have they found Mark yet?"

The officers pause, exchange a look, and turn back at her.

"Excuse me?" one of them says.

"My friend from school, Mark Stevens. Do you know whether they found him?"

"Do you know Mark?"

"I..." I see her decide what to divulge, and I am impressed that she chooses to be prudent. "I am his friend."

"We are still looking for him," the other officer says.

"That's been two nights now, hasn't it?"

"Yes."

"And you have no idea where he is?"

"At the moment, we are looking everywhere we can. We have a group of volunteers. Maybe after school, you could help them."

I have a sudden idea – an idea of how to both appease my darling Flora and demonstrate my wealth.

"What if you were to have more funding for the volunteers? Would that help?"

"That would certainly help more people come forward, yes."

I open a drawer and take out my cheque book.

"I would like to make a donation to the effort, if you please."

"Really? That is very kind."

"Not at all. Would thirty thousand pounds help?"

They exchange a glance.

"Really, Mr Brittle, if you cannot afford that..."

"Oh, don't judge me by this house. It's only temporary. I assure you I am quite wealthy."

I hand them the cheque.

"Well, thank you. We will be sure to pass this on to the volunteers and see what we can do."

"And we will get back to you about your wife as soon as we've found anything," says the other officer, though I honestly couldn't care less.

"Thank you," I say, as is customary when someone offers to do what they believe is a favour. When they have left, I return to Flora and look at her.

She looks back at me and I honestly cannot read her expression.

"That's a lot of money," she says.

"It's less than pennies to me, Flora," I tell her, and lean across the kitchen side. "We can have the kind of life that people only dream of. If you let us, that is."

"Yesterday you said you would kill me."

"If you breathe a word of what happened, yes, I will. In the most invasive and violating of ways. But that isn't going to happen, is it?"

She doesn't react.

"Is it?" I repeat, painting my voice with anger.

"No," she answers.

"We are going to be happy, aren't we?"

"Yes," she finally replies.

"Good. Now come back from school straight away."

"And if I don't?"

I mull over the question.

"I would not even wish to entertain the thought."

"And if I do? What then? Are you going to hurt me again?"

"Again? What is this *again*? I have never hurt you!"

She looks to wipe away tears again. She looks down and does not look up, and I reach across and wipe the tear away.

"Now we'll have none of that," I tell her, and though my voice is comforting it is not, and she knows that. "By the time you get home I expect you to be grateful, to be happy for the life we are going to lead."

She cries harder.

"Flora, stop it."

She doesn't.

"*Stop it!*"

She wants to cry some more, but she stops and holds her breath, scrunches up her face, does all she can to cease her grief.

"That's better," I say.

She stands. She still hasn't eaten her cereal.

"Are you not going to finish your breakfast?"

Her body retreats in on itself and she shakes her head.

"I'm going to go to school," she says with minimal assurance, yet she doesn't move. She just hovers.

"Okay."

"If I didn't tell anyone..." she says, her voice muffled and small. "If I was to keep it to myself... then... would you... let me go?"

Let me go?

The question incenses me. It implies I am keeping her captive, and I am not, we are having a wonderful life, and I am looking forward to living it dammit!

"I would not let you go, Flora, as there is nothing to let you go from," I say with as much calmness as I can, but I feel my hands tearing up a kitchen roll I have somehow acquired.

She takes a big, deep breath, and nods timidly.

"Have a good day," I tell her, slowly and methodically, deep and gravely, ensuring she knows that I am not happy with her implications.

She walks with small steps and her head down, so different to the confident, sexy sway she normally has, and as she disappears out of the door. I wonder whether she is still the same Flora I have come to feel so close to.

Or whether she is someone else altogether.

Someone who I will come to detest, rather than care for as I do.

And I hope, for her sake, that this is not the case.

22

I STOP off at a hidden away, high-class restaurant named Gustuchio's, a few miles off junction seven of the M5.

I engage in a rather triumphant mackerel with pesto and garlic and herbs. It may not sound delightful, but believe me, it is.

I send my empty plate away and request a dessert menu just as my mobile phone rings. Normally I would not answer it, but on this occasion, it is Flora's school and my mind begins to race.

Did they see me loitering around the other day?

Have they linked me with Mark's disappearance?

Or, God forbid, (even though I am not a believer in an omnipotent, higher being fabricated from unintelligent human minds, I feel this is an appropriate turn of phrase in this scenario), has Flora told them?

Has she betrayed my trust?

But if she had, why ever would they call me?

Unless it was some kind of trap. A setup I will step into believing that I am unfounded only to be led away in hand-cuffs, disgraced before I am fully able to enjoy the benefits of my wealth.

Realising the phone is about to ring out, I put it to my ear and, despite how much I detest people talking on their phones in restaurants, I answer it.

"Hello?"

"Hello, is that Mr Brittle?" asks a stern female voice that I imagine being attached to a stern overweight black woman.

"Yes..."

"This is Flora's school calling. We have been unable to get hold of Flora's mother, so we've called you, I hope that's okay."

No, you haven't.

And it doesn't sound like you know why.

"Yes, that is absolutely fine. How can I be of service?"

It's best to remain jovial and not force yourself to presumptions in situations like these.

"Well, Flora has been a little... off, today. Her behaviour has been unacceptable and a little alarming, to say the least."

"How so?"

"It is best if we speak face to face. I have Flora working in isolation with me, are you able to come in now?"

Oh, what has that dreadful girl done now? All I have done for her and she repays me with futile distractions.

"Is it really necessary?" I ask.

"Oh, I'm afraid so, Mr Brittle."

Oh balls.

"Fine, I will leave now."

"I appreciate that, we will see you soon."

I hang up without saying goodbye and look over an exquisite dessert menu that has just been handed to me.

Crème Brule, Tia Mesu, profiteroles draped in chocolate and honey...

There is even an option to have a tray selection of

desserts, a smaller portion of each rather than having to choose one in particular.

I curse this menu for temptation, for showing me what I am now unable to have. I do not hide my irritation as I hand the menu back and request the bill.

"Are the options not to your satisfactory, sir?"

Oh, stop calling me sir, I hate it. It's such nonsense. I am no more a sir than you are a madam; you only call me this because you get paid to do so rather than any kind of real formal respect. Just talk to me normally and be done with it.

"It's not that, it's just something has come up and I need to go."

"Oh, I am sorry to hear that."

No, you're not; again, stop it.

I do not tip, and I leave with haste. I return my car to the road and drive up the motorway, wondering what she has done now. This is a time to be avoiding distractions, not a time to be attracting all the unwanted attention you can.

When I arrive, I am led to the headmistress's office, and the corridors are just as depressing and hopeless as the ground outside them. Corridors lined with lockers and classrooms with teenagers sat in lines feels too much like organised punishment, as if they were incarcerated rather than learning about the world.

The woman is not black, as I imagined, though she is stocky. She has red cheeks and curly hair that waddles from side to side and I cannot figure out how someone could physically have sex with her.

Flora is sat outside the office, and she glances at me, sitting there all slouched with her arms folded, but the woman suggests we speak alone.

"Please, allow me to get to the point straight away," she says, and I'm not stopping you, you daft mare. "A student earlier on was asked to read out a poem in class that she had written about her mother. In the middle of this poem, Flora stood up and stormed out with her face in her hands and tears streaming down her cheeks. She refused to tell a teacher why this is."

Annoying, yes, that she caused such unnecessary attention.

But, good girl for not telling them why you felt the need to have such an outburst.

"It's not all," the woman says, pulling a concerned face like those teachers who pretend to be all caring do. My best teacher at school was an arsehole who spent most of his time belittling those that refused to do what he said. I liked him though, it built character. "Flora was sat in my office crying, again refusing to tell me why, then the girl who read the poem came in to check if Flora was okay."

There is a long pause and I feel as if I'm supposed to interject.

"That was... nice... of her..."

Is that what I'm supposed to say?

"Yes, yes it was," she says, as if she is a detective who is suspicious of something, and not the failed Master of Education she always wished she was. "But then Flora attacked this girl."

"Attacked?" I repeat. Flora has never so much as slapped a girl, despite many times when there have been some nasty pieces of work well deserving of it.

"She pulled her hair, slammed her head on the table, and attempted to put her head in the sink where she tried to pour water on her. It took six teachers to intervene and stop her."

Well, well.

My Flora.

Who'd have known?

"Do you have any idea why she may have acted in this way?"

"Her mother," I reply, as matter-of-factly as I can manage, "did not return home last night. She is still missing."

"Ah," the woman says, sitting back like it all makes sense. "We were not aware of this."

"No. No, you were not."

"Is it the best idea her being in school during such a terrible time?"

I sigh, annoyed at the impudence.

"I feel it necessary for her to continue as normal, and I do not feel it necessary for you to give me unsolicited advice."

"Forgive me, I am just trying to think of what's best for Flora."

"I will talk to her."

"I really think further punishment is needed for what she did to the girl. She only came to apologise."

"Why?"

The woman looks stumped.

"Excuse me?" she says.

"I said I'd talk to her."

"But we need to do something our end."

"Why?"

"Why? Because I have a duty of care to my students to make sure they are safe, and if someone attacks someone so violently, then we have to make sure it's known that it is not acceptable."

"I said I'd talk to her."

"I am aware of this, but I believe a five-day suspension will suffice, then we will have a meeting before she returns."

I am stunned.

Gobsmacked, astonished, and dumbfounded.

How on earth am I going to eat where I wish to, and go about my business as I like, with her in the way?

Then I realise it may not be so bad to show Flora the life-style that she will now become accustomed to.

Once she tastes that mackerel and sees that dessert menu she will forget all about her stupid mother and pledge herself to her new life as a rich who-gives-a-fuck woman.

"So be it," I say, and rise as I decide this meeting is over.

She rises too and I'm already at the door when I realise she is offering to shake my hand, so I ignore it.

I step outside and I look at Flora.

She looks up at me, still crying.

I don't know whether to tell her to get a grip or to hug her with pride.

Instead, I just say, "Get in the car."

I walk and she follows, and we drive away from this wretched place.

23

————

WE BEGIN the car journey in an equanimous silence – or, at least, I do.

Flora, however, is stewing. I can feel the heat of her anger glowering at me. She sits low in her chair with her arms folded, all negative body language if my reading is correct, and her face is something to behold; dragged downwards so much she looks like that old cartoon character I used to watch as a child... who was it... ah, yes. Droopy.

She looks like Droopy.

I chuckle to myself and feel her scowl, and even though her scowl is not in my direction, I still feel like it's a scowl for me.

"We were supposed to be avoiding attention, weren't we?" I say, finally terminating the silence as we pull up at a red light. In the lane to my left is a man with glasses from the eighties and a tie from the future. I admire how he dresses, then I don't. It seemed interesting at first and it made me inquisitive, now I feel it's a droll attempt at being original. I decide that I dislike this man.

My inner dialogue ceases as I realise Flora has not answered me.

"Flora, it is not kind to ignore someone."

She says something, and her voice is so small and so tender it's like she's a timid little girl hidden away in a box, and she's not a timid little girl, she's a fiercely wild sex-craving minx.

I stare at her to indicate that I did not quite catch what she said, and she repeats with a voice just about audible for my ear's perception.

"Do you even feel bad?" she asks.

Feel bad? What, about picking her up from school? It was what I was requested to do by her headmistress. I don't quite know what I would feel bad about.

I decide to inquire further.

"About what?"

"You know what."

"No, Flora, I honestly do not. Please elaborate."

She turns and looks at me and never has she appeared more like a petulant teenager.

"Mum," she says, and it takes me a moment, and I realise she is still referring to the incident from the previous afternoon. I thought we were done with that, and I find it quite irritating, but I must remember that she is different and she may not quite have come down off the adrenaline yet.

"What of it?" I ask.

"What you did to her," she says, then corrects herself: "What *we* did to her."

Ah, yes.

This is what I hoped for.

By involving her she now feels partially responsible. She has not said anything to anyone today, which means she cannot claim she was coerced, considering she has not admitted what we did – (one thing that I should praise her for, and I make a mental note to do so) – and she also feels responsible. She was there, she helped, did as I instructed. Most likely out of fear, yes, but at no point did she run and with the lawyers I can afford they would batter that point right into a jury.

"You did well today," I say, as a sudden burst rather than a well-articulated sentence, and I regret the way my desperation to offer her some positive reinforcement has skewed my ability to form semantics.

I try again, this time slower.

"I mean, aside from drawing unneeded attention to yourself with your foolish yet oddly admirable shenanigans, you did well. You said nothing, and you showed that I can trust you. And that's real progress, really it is."

I put my hand on her leg and she flinches and I do not like that she flinches.

Before I can say anything about it, a sudden smell wafts over me, like rotting, and I wonder what on earth is wrong with my car. I must remember to get a new air freshener and just as I think this thought the petrol light comes on and beeps at me with three assertive electronic noises.

There is a petrol station ahead, and so I pull in. It is empty and I pull into the first bay, kill the engine, and turn to Flora, reaching my hand across and putting it in her hair. She tries to move out of my reach, so I grab her hair and force her to be still. Once she cooperates, I stroke her hair instead.

See, I can be affectionate.

"What would you like for tea tonight?" I ask. "Anything, I will get it."

She frowns at me.

"Sooner or later you need to stop this attitude, Flora."

"You really don't get why I'm upset, do you?"

"I have been wondering."

"You really can't understand any part of human emotion, can you?"

I sigh. "I struggle to comprehend some aspects of human nature, but that is only because my intellect is far more advanced. I do try, Flora, but if you are feeling a certain way you need to spell it out for me so I can understand."

She shakes her head. The tears are back.

Those bloody tears.

What purpose do they serve? And why do they keep reoccurring?

"Flora, this needs to stop," I say. "Your behaviour has been most erratic."

"Are you going to kill me too?" she asks, a sudden change of tone.

"Why, what would make you think that?"

"Because you said you would."

"Only if you spoil things for us, Flora."

"What if this is not what I want? What if I didn't want to... What if I..."

She struggles to end the sentence and she cries again.

"How would some wine sound?"

She wants to say something, I can see it, her face is too tense, but something stops her. Fear, maybe. Awareness of how impatient I am growing.

I step out the car. I need a moment.

I fill the tank with petrol and decide that she can choose the wine. That would be a nice thing for her, would it not?

And so I tell her this, to no gratitude in return, and we walk into the store. I pick up some bread, the most expensive loaf they have, though expensive would be a farfetched way to describe anything in here.

I take her to the wine section and she doesn't pick one, so I pick one for her.

We take the items to the counter, and the acne-ridden teenager bags them for us.

"Take these to the car," I say, thinking some responsibility may make her feel valued. "Put them in the boot for me."

And, as I take out my wallet, she does as I ask.

She walks to the car as I hand over my credit card.

She goes to the boot, presses down the button, and opens it.

And that is the point I remember.

And the reason to that odorous whiff becomes so pertinently clear my hand freezes over the pin-pad.

Mark is still in the boot.

24

Mark.

Fucking Mark.

Fucking fucking Mark.

She opens the boot and she can't move and I can't get to her quick enough. I batter in my pin number, ignoring the offer of a receipt, and rush to the car.

She is just turning to run as I grab her wrist and pull her close, so close that no one will notice my restraining her.

The boot is open and Mark's eyes stare up at me. His face is pale and discoloured and some kind of bloody foam seems to have come from his nose and his mouth. He smells like something fierce, something I cannot quite articulate into a succinct set of words for you, my dear voyeur, to quite comprehend. If you have never been near a dead body after a few days then you cannot quite understand the smells it contains, and it surprises me that this odour did not alert me more as I drove.

Now, it is immense. The boot seems to have contained it, and now the smell is unleashed. I look around to see if anyone has noticed.

No one seems to. One guy holds his nose but looks around helplessly for the source. I look up and the CCTV is on the other side of the car, pointing into the petrol station, and there is one by the shop front but not one that seems to be in any way directed at this car.

I close the boot, thankful that this slip up has not cost me more dearly than the perturbed look on Flora's face.

She tries to pull herself from my grip so I grip tighter, tight enough that her wrist turns purple. She is crying again, but at least she is now being quiet about it. She stares at me in a way she has never stared before, like she sees someone other than me, like I am not the person she has known and fucked behind her mother's back.

"Please, let me go," she whimpers.

"You don't want to go," I tell her.

"I'll scream."

"You'll scream?" I can't help but grin. "Go ahead. You'll be a non-discreetly petulant teenager who doesn't like that they've been suspended from school, and I will see it as a case of distrust and ensure that you suffer the same fate as Mark."

"Why are you doing this to me?"

"I am not doing anything to you."

If anything, it is Mark I have done something to.

"Please, just let me go."

She tries to pull her arm away again but I can see her hand has gone numb and she can do little to remove herself from my grasp.

I look over my shoulder and the teenager at the checkout inside the station is staring. I smile and nod and hope that he minds his own fucking business.

"I did this for you," I tell her.

"What?"

"He made you cry. I saw it."

"You were spying on me?"

"Oh, please. The way you were flaunting Mark about, did you really expect not to incite any jealousy? I presumed that was the purpose to your incessant texting."

"I was texting because he was a boy I liked. And you were married to my mum, and if anything had reason to prompt jealousy, it was that."

She has a point.

"But he hurt you. He upset you."

"Because he's gay!"

"Well, I did not know that at the time. Did I?"

She tries to pull her arm away again, so I tighten.

"I won't tell anyone," she lies. "I won't. Please, I'll just run, and we never have to see each other again."

Now that hurts.

I feel my heart shatter and splinter into too many pieces for her to ever be able to put together again.

It is in this moment, in this extraordinary claim, that I realise: Flora does not want the same things as I do.

All these things I've done for her have been for nothing.

She's an ungrateful wretch and a cow and a fiend and I have gone to all this trouble for us to have a great life, and she has gone and blown it all in one little sentence.

She never wants to see me again.

I repeat it to myself over and over, and each time it stings just that little bit more.

But I am ready to give her one more chance.

It will be on my terms. And it will not be as she wishes.

"Get in the car," I tell her.

"No," she says, though it lacks conviction and it's so pathetic it barely registers.

"Get in the car or I will gut you."

She finally complies and I walk to the door with her,

opening it and seeing her in. I do not remove my eyes from her as I take myself to the driver's side.

We resume the silence we had at the beginning of the car journey, but this silence is different. It is more morbid, more sinister. It is the silence of heartache, of pain, of dreading the sad future that is to befall us.

I can't believe that it has come to this, that I must force upon her the doting characteristics that she should so willingly have already given.

When we arrive home, I take my car inside the garage and kill the engine and neither of us move. We just sit there, caught in the midst of whatever hurt has been caused.

Why, dear voyeur, do you assume that I feel nothing?

Is it because you see me as dissimilar to you, or that I have killed three people to date?

Never forget, I am not dissimilar to you. In fact, I am you – just the version of you where you are not contained by the conditioning society has instilled on you since birth.

You are put into school and told how to think, what to do, and taught to know right from wrong even though right and wrong do not exist. A lion killing its prey is not seen as wrong, yet a human doing it is?

Come off it.

We are animals, all of us.

We can domesticize ourselves as much as we think, but our animalistic urges will not be contained.

We want to kill.

We want to hunt.

We want to fuck.

And that is all we are.

I get out of the car and retrieve a large bicycle chain that I used during my bike phase several years ago. I thought I could conform to society's standards and expectations by finding a way to push my urge into exercise.

See, I was like you once – trying to direct my impulses into something considered the norm.

I take the padlock off Lisa's bike that she still claims to use – sorry, *claimed* to use – and I walk to the passenger side, open the car door, and look at Flora looking back at me.

"Get out," I tell her.

She shakes her head.

"I said get out," I repeat, dumbfounded by her insolence.

"Please..."

Oh, this again.

I grab her arm and I drag her out. After ensuring I have locked the car, I pull her into the house and through the living room. She puts up a small fight, trying to pull her arm away and pulling on my grip, but I only tighten it and this only hurts her more.

I kick open the door to the basement.

"No, please, no!"

She resists too much and I can't get her in.

I throw the bicycle chain and padlock down the stairs and use my now spare hand to grab the back her hair and, with all my strength, I drag her down the steps. She pulls and ends up falling and batting her knees on each of the steps on the way down.

I throw her to the floor and mount her so my head is over her feet before she can resume her fight.

She struggles and kicks and thrashes but I manage to pin on ankle down, put the chain around it as tightly as I can manage, and use the padlock to lock it into place.

I find another padlock Lisa used to lock a drawer containing what she called our *important papers*. I tie the other side of the chain around a large metal radiator and use the padlock to secure it. I always thought it was ridiculous to include a radiator in your basement, but it has finally served its purpose.

I stand back and admire my work and she is laying there, tugging on the chain to no avail, trying to wriggle her ankle out of it to find it doesn't even move.

And, eventually, she stops.

Looks up at me.

So weak and so vulnerable.

And, honestly, despite the sadness of my having to do this, the sight arouses me. Flora chained up and submissive, ready for me to dominate her.

I walk over to her and crouch beside her, take hold of her chin and pull her head closer to mine.

I go to kiss her and she bites my lip and pulls away.

I taste blood.

Honestly, I know I should be angry, but it only turns me on more.

I place my hand on her leg and run it up her thigh and she bats it away.

I try to mount her and she struggles out of my grasp.

"Leave me alone!"

Now this is not what I expected.

"Don't touch me! I don't ever want to be near you again!"

Oh, Flora, if your wish to runaway hurt, then it was nothing compared to this hurt now.

Which makes it even more important that I persist.

Because I know you feel it when I'm inside of you, I know you do, and I know you will stop saying all these hurtful things when you feel it again.

But, just as I grab hold of her hair and begin to turn her over, I am distracted by a loud knock on the front door.

Flora screams out an almighty scream, screeching and

shrieking and pounding against my eardrums with such ferocity that it gives me a headache.

I grab a towel or a cloth or whatever it is and tie it around her mouth to muffle the sound.

Now her arms... What of her arms...

I search for a rope, but I cannot find any.

She wriggles out of the towel/cloth.

The knock comes again.

I guess I'll just have to rely on the security of the basement's sound proofing. Whoever it is, I will keep them on the front porch, or in the kitchen should it be necessary, the room furthest away from the basement, and the room with knives that I can use to dispose of whoever it is should they grow suspicious.

She continues to scream as I go up the stairs. I do not leave a light on for her as she does not deserve it.

I close the door and listen. Her screams are only mildly audible. I should be fine.

Hopefully.

Those knocks repeat again.

I walk through the living room and peer out of the window.

I see them.

My mind goes to a bad place, but I remind myself that I shouldn't jump to assumptions.

There could be any reason why a police car is parked on my drive.

25

MY FIRST INSTINCT is to glance at the knives in the kitchen and decide whether to get one and hide it or just keep it in arm's reach.

Then I remember, these are police.

They are trained to deal with untrained assailants with knives. They have tasers, pepper sprays, asps, and there are two of them who have been in far more fights than I've ever been in.

And, even if I did manage to overpower them in some miraculous occurrence, what then?

Killing a police officer is different.

Kill a kid, their parents will cry.

Kill an officer, every other officer will be after you. And they will not treat you well when you get arrested, and when they get you back to the station, there will be a few eyes looking the other way...

No.

I am just going to rely on my cunning and my wit to outsmart them.

And, failing that, the most expensive lawyers money can buy.

I put my hand on the door handle, ready my mind, and open it. I feign surprise.

"Officers," I say. "Is everything okay?"

"Good morning Mr Brittle, we are here about your wife," one of them says, and I sigh a huge sigh of relief.

I have not been caught. Of course, I haven't. I was careful, methodical, smart. I outwit an evidence hunter with ease. Forgetting about the dead body in the boot of my car aside, I am not an idiot.

Besides, that body was different – I was so distracted by the disposal of Lisa I forgot about Mark. It will not happen again.

"May we come in?" the officer asks, and I notice they are both carrying their hats, and they have stretched, solemn faces.

"Yes," I say, and usher them in. I guide them to the kitchen where I pause, and listen to see if Flora can be heard.

As it is, she cannot.

"We have some news," says the officer who hasn't spoken yet. "Maybe it would be best to be sat down?"

I don't really wish to sit down but I do not want to seem difficult, so I take a seat at the kitchen counter.

"We have found what we believe to be your wife's body," he says, and I open my mouth with shock.

"We believe she may have taken her own life," says the other, so sad, and I look sad whilst on the inside I am jumping for joy.

They think it's suicide.

How stupefyingly wonderfully marvellous.

"How?" I ask, stretching out the vowel sound.

"She drove her car into her lake and drowned."

"Are you sure it was suicide? She would never hurt herself!"

"We still have to receive the report from the coroner, but there are no obvious lacerations that suggest an attack."

I banged her head, didn't I?

Will they find that?

Then again, she could have banged her head as the car went into the lake. I think I may be clear on that one.

"Well..." I really wish they would go now, but I need to maintain the performance. I put my hand to my chin and stare off into the distance. I think about attempting to conjure tears, but I know I would fail to do so.

"Is there anyone you would like us to speak to? Anyone else you would like us to contact on your behalf?"

"No, no thank you."

"We may need you to confirm her identity. Would that be okay?"

"Yes. Yes, I guess."

Urgh. I don't want to see her again.

One of the officers puts a leaflet entitled *Grief* on the kitchen side. The image is of a young black man in a shirt and wearing glasses with his hand on the back of some white woman with her head in her hands.

"There are some numbers here you can call, should you need it."

They do that sad smile people do and turn toward the door.

And then they stop.

Turn and look at me.

"Is everything okay, Mr Brittle?" one of them asks.

"Well, it's sad news..."

"I mean, that noise. It sounds..."

Now I hear it. Clanging against a radiator and banging against a wall.

Flora.

"That would be my stepdaughter. She's sorting out some things in the basement."

It continues, constant clanging.

"Is she okay?"

"Yes, I will go see to her now."

"Do you need us to help with letting her know–"

"I am her legal guardian, thank you, I am sure I will be quite fine."

It's getting louder.

They pause and hold my gaze, and for a moment I think they are not going to leave.

Then they do.

I wait for their car to go, listening to the constant wave of noise, then I charge to the basement door, down the stairs, and find her banging her chains repeatedly against the radiator.

I put my hand around her neck, pick her up and shove her against the wall.

I look into her eyes, deep into them, and I see dread, I see fear, I see spite and anger and, worst of all, I see her mother.

"Go ahead," she says. "Kill me. You may as well."

Is that what's happened?

I've made her life so unbearable that she is now not scared of the threat of death.

She hates me now, I can tell.

But she loved me once, and she will love me again.

What I need is a house where she can roam free yet have no way of escaping.

A mansion with means of trapping her inside.

Somewhere she can remain unchained, but I will know she will not run from me.

I do not wish to kill her, and I am desperately looking for alternatives, and I just hope my options do not run out.

Maybe we just need to be rid of this house, be gone from the place where we were both repressed by that dreaded woman.

And the sooner I find us a new home, the happier we'll be.

26

I use Lisa's old laptop to scour the internet.

I despise the internet, and I despise computers, and I despise technology.

Actually, that may be a little hasty.

Today's technology, I despise.

If it were up to me, I'd take all technology back to where it was in 1995 and freeze it. That was the optimum time for technology. We had computers, and they had an operating system that allowed us to type on a word processor and we had phones that you connected to the wall and used to communicate with people.

Nowadays we have computers that can run tasks that people would be better off doing in person.

We have emails that you will send across the office to a colleague working metres away instead of getting up and entering conversation with them.

We have self-service machines that say the same thing every time I use them and have an extreme dislike for any unexpected item in the bagging area that is entirely expected as I damn well put it there.

And we have social media, a drain on the human soul, an ADHD-fuelling fad that involves people posting pictures of food instead of eating it and getting involved with people they don't know.

Don't get me wrong, I wilfully go along with advancements that helps me avoid interaction with inept idiots every moment of my day, but this has gone too far.

And, before you say it, yes, social media would be a perfect way to find prospectives to help me engage with my burning needs, the needs I embrace and you deny. But there's always a damn trace on everything you do.

Google should help solve all problems, but if I type into Google *how do I dispose of a dead body,* then there's solid evidence that would damn any testimony I may give to the contrary.

But, alas, it has its use for my current needs, and that allows me to find it a little more tolerable. After all, I have just discovered a house that seems perfect, and I would not have found it had it not been for this inducer of catatonic teenagers we label a machine.

So here I stand, a break from the banging and the shouting in the basement – honestly, that girl has a set of lungs on her; which makes me wonder why she never used those lungs to scream while I was fucking her and whether I was not quite doing enough to make her scream but, then again, maybe she's just not a sex screamer, after all, they say *the louder the gobshite the worse they are at night,* not that we ever fornicated at night because of Lisa's unwelcome presence – anyway, I digress, and I forget where I was.

Ah, yes, I was taking a welcome break from the chaotic noise from beneath me. I decide to leave in order to view this house I have just discovered that may just be ideal.

I drive down the road and it's like a road I didn't know

existed. Houses of various sizes, and by this I mean various sizes of *huge*, and a nice, wide, vacant road to peruse them.

I pull up outside a large set of gates. I can barely see the house it is that far back from the road, which is damn near perfect – no one would hear Flora's screams, and she can exercise that set of lungs however much she wishes.

I step out of the car and a tiny woman with a brown pony-tail and glasses half the size of her face walks up to me.

"You must be Mr Brittle," she says, and her voice sounds far too big for such a tiny body.

"I am."

"Lovely to meet you, I am Mary Lamb."

She offers a hand and I reluctantly shake it, as is the bizarre custom.

I mull over the words to *Mary had a little lamb* in my mind, wondering if that was the inspiration for such a ludicrous term for a person.

"Shall we?" she says, and she is too smiley and too happy and I know she's trying to sell me something, I just wish she knew her clientele. Yes, if I were a young couple in their twenties buying their first house then wonderful, you are smiling just the right amount.

But I am not.

I am a murderer with little patience and a detest of people that comes out of a lack of ability to understand them.

Adapt, you wretched beast.

"It's quite a long driveway," she tells me, and on the one hand I'm thrilled as I want a massive drive, on the other hand I'm disappointed as this means she will force small talk as we walk down it.

"So did you find the place okay?" she asks, and what a ridiculous question.

Of course I have found it okay.

I would not be here if I had not found it okay.

I would still be out there looking for it, you fool.

"Yes," I say without looking at her, hoping that she takes the hint.

She seems to.

The driveway is wide and surrounded by lavish bushes perfectly cut and overarching trees decorating the drive. It will need a gardener, but that's okay – it's not like the money's going anywhere.

When we eventually reach the house, I cannot help but be impressed. Seven floors high and so wide I cannot see one end from the other. It is not a new build – in fact, the architecture is rather classical. As we walk inside, I can see that whilst the grand staircase and a few pieces of furniture retain that classical look, the living room and kitchen space is quite modern.

And that's just the first floor.

"There is something I do need to show you," that Mary Lamb woman says, interrupting my moment of ecstasy as I marvel at this perfect dwelling.

She takes me to the back door and to a switch.

"What's this?" I ask.

"The last person who lived here was an army veteran, and he suffered quite severely with post-traumatic stress disorder. I don't know if you've heard of it?"

Yes, of course I've heard of it, you quisquilian.

I allow my silence to confirm, and she continues as if it didn't even matter.

"He ended up paying a lot of money to have shutters installed as a result of his paranoia. He very much believed someone was going to come and attack him."

"Show me," I say, too eager to see.

She presses the switch and metal shutters descend around

every window, and I can hear them throughout the house, blessing it with darkness, an impenetrable fort.

As soon as they are down I open a window and try to batter at it, but it is solid, unbeatable.

It is perfect.

And I can't quite believe my fortitude.

How I managed to find such a place...

Maybe that computer does have its uses...

How wonderful. Magnificent. Awe-inspiring.

A figment of imagination that even my wild imagination couldn't conjure.

She must think my open jaw is negative shock, as she starts to say how they are prepared to remove the shutters for any prospective buyers.

"You will do no such thing," I say.

"The reason I show you this," she continues, and I'm not really listening, "is as an explanation for something we have to be honest with. This ex-soldier did kill himself in this house. He–"

"I don't care," I say.

She is momentarily stumped, but the incessant smile returns.

"Would you like to see the other floors?"

"No. I'll take it."

"You mean you'll put in an offer?"

"I will offer you twenty percent above asking price."

"Well... are you sure? Do you not wish to think it over?"

"I just said I wish to purchase it."

She looks gobsmacked, and I'm not quite sure she believes me. I look at her and show her how serious I am, and I believe it starts to register.

"Well, we can put you in touch with our financial advisors, and we can start to get the mortgage–"

"I don't need a mortgage."

She is stunned again.

"Excuse me?"

"I said I don't need a mortgage. I will pay cash."

"Cash? Do you know how much–"

"I will pay cash. I can transfer it now if you wish, or in notes if you have enough space to store it. Either way, I wish to move in by the end of the week."

She says she is not sure if that's possible but, within the hour, I have sent her the money and we go back to her office and sign all the appropriate papers.

A sure sign that, as I am about to learn now I can truly flaunt my wealth, money can buy just about anything.

27

WHEN I GET HOME – though it will not be my home much longer – I go onto the internet and I order my next essential purchase and arrange for their delivery the day after we move in.

A group of four healthy adult pigs.

Animals to dispose of Fucking Mark's body, and of any further bodies that may be created.

Although I fear that waiting until Friday will be quite a challenge. My car and my garage truly are starting to stink now. What's more, it may be noticed by the removal company that I also order via the internet.

It has been quite a few days since Mark's living body ceased to live and his corpse was created. It's as if there is rotting meat getting further and further past its expiry date.

Which it is, I suppose.

What's more, there are various forms of life crawling over him and growing inside of him now. And he keeps releasing gases as his body decompresses all the air it previously held inside.

This is the not-so-fun part, I must admit.

The part I do wish I could do without.

But, alas, even after a wonderful session of sex one must get a tissue and wipe up the remnants.

The same goes with this.

Unfortunately, every act of bliss is followed by the act of cleaning up.

Either way, I am very much concerned that my car is going to pick up the odours and I will never get them out. For such a wonderful car – it has Bluetooth after all – it would be a shame to wreck its wonderful pristine interior smell. I worry, in fact, that the odour has already worked away at it quite considerably, and I doubt that the boot will ever be the same.

So I wonder where to store the body.

And the answer comes to me quite clearly. It's obvious really, isn't it?

Flora cared quite deeply about Mark. Evidently, from her excessive reaction. Maybe she would like to spend some more time with him. Maybe she would like a chance to say good-bye, to confess her last confessions.

I will be doing her a favour, and hopefully this will reduce the chances of me having to kill her, because, really, she is starting to make things look that way with all the banging and the screaming.

I ensure every curtain of the house is closed without any gaps, so all actions are obscured from the neighbours.

Then I take Mark, place him in a large black bag I would have previously used for the dustbin, and tie the bag up at the end. This ensures that I leave no evidence on the tufts of the carpet or the cracks of the kitchen tiles.

From there, I drag him through to the basement door, and I pause.

It's like delivering a birthday cake. You know you're about

to sing Happy Birthday and that the child will be all surprised and they will blow out their candles.

I can't wait for her to see what I have!

I open the door and I call down to her, "Flora! I have a surprise for you!"

She goes silent. Her screaming and banging seems to cease, and I can suddenly remember what it's like to enjoy quiet again.

I drag the bag down the stairs to the basement.

She backs up against the radiator, and she stares wide eyed at the bag. There is a stink of piss and her skirt is stained and I realise I forgot to get her a pot.

Ah well, this will make up for it.

"Now, I know you cared for Mark," I say, grinning wildly, bursting with excitement. "And you know I am going to have to be rid of his body. Ooh, that reminds me! We are moving to a new house this Friday, one where you can roam around without the chains. Of course, you will be trapped in, but there're seven floors and plenty of space."

She looks at me like I'm taking gibberish.

I ignore it.

"Anyway, until then, I was trying to think of what to do with Mark, and I thought, you might like to spend the last day or two with him. Would you like that?"

She gags.

It's the smell, I know.

But it's fine.

I open the bag and take his face out and she more than gags: she turns and retches and vomits blood and bile all over the basement floor.

"Oh, Flora," I say. This isn't very attractive.

But I must be understanding.

I step toward her, going to reach my hand out, to make an

effort, and she recoils. She actually flinches away, has the audacity to move as far away as the bicycle chain will allow.

"Well, really," I exclaim. "I do this for you! I am understanding about your affections toward another man, and... Flora, I do not understand. What is it you want?"

"Please do not leave that in here with me."

"That?"

"Please just – just – just take it elsewhere."

I am stumped.

I thought she'd appreciate it...

Oh, she is a complicated one, my Flora.

"Well what should I do with it?"

"I don't know, just... please... take it..."

The only other option is if I take it to the farm like I did Carluccio, but first I will need to hack him up.

"Fine, give me a minute," I say, and I go and retrieve a saw and an axe.

I would ask her to help, but I'm not quite sure I trust her with the weapons yet.

So I hack and saw and hack and saw and it's quite tough, you know.

Flora looks away for the entire time. I think she's sick again, but I ignore it, and as I go about my activity – on *her wishes*, don't forget – I wonder about her.

And I contain my annoyance that my gift was rejected.

Maybe she just wanted to leave Mark in the past.

After all, I want to forget about Lisa. So why shouldn't she want to forget about her ex?

And, with that thought, I realise just how selfish and inconsiderate I'd been.

So, once I have the pieces hacked up and in the bag which takes me well over the hour, I move them into the boot of my car for transportation. I get a cloth, return to the basement, and I stand before her.

She looks up at me with that face and I've never seen her looking so vulnerable.

I walk to her and she tries to flinch away, but she needs me, and so I grab her, and I pull her close, and I dab at the loose strands of sick that remain on her chin.

She stares up at me with wide eyes, though not quite as wide as Mark's, but more alive, and I look back at them and think about how much we have to look forward to.

"I wasn't lying about the new house, you know," I tell her, keeping my voice lucid and mellow. "It's got seven floors, a large driveway, gardens, it's wonderful. And it has shutters that block any escape, so I can leave you there without having to worry about this silly little chain. Would you like that? To be able to run around a bit more?"

She doesn't say anything. Just continues that stare.

I forget, I should perhaps apologise.

It is one of the few customs of society I actually think serves a purpose.

"I am sorry. I didn't think. I want to forget my past, and I know you want to forget yours, and start anew, and I shouldn't have brought Mark down here. It doesn't help, and I know that now, and it will never happen again."

I pretend that she smiles, even though she doesn't.

But she doesn't need to.

Because in my mind she thanks me incessantly, and she wants to kiss me, but I tell her to wait, as it will be more special in the new house.

"I will go get you some food," I tell her. "And some water to wash down any sick left in your throat. And a mop for all of this."

173

I stop wiping her face and I stroke her hair instead, slowly, firmly.

"Friday, Flora. Just wait until Friday. Then we can be happy, like we always wanted."

She closes her eyes and I have to turn away because, I swear, if I see her cry again my mood is going to change instantly.

I kiss her forehead and I turn to leave.

I pause at the bottom of the steps.

I look at her.

"I really want us to be happy," I tell her. "I hope you do too."

And I leave to go get her some tea before I take Mark to the pigs at the farm. I empty the bag into a troth, and I go unnoticed once again.

It's almost getting too easy, you know.

And, as the urge lifts back up from my stomach and settles into my mind, I realise that, soon, I will need to kill again.

I HAVE TO

I HAVE to bide my time.

I have to think clearly.

I have to bear it.

I have to forget about my mother's dead eyes looking up at me, forget watching her car trickle over the pier while I did nothing.

I did nothing.

Nothing.

I have to live with that.

I have to survive, because she would want me to survive.

Because right now, death's looking pretty good. It's never been far from my fate, I've always dabbled in depression, but never fully explored the passion.

He says we are moving to a new house.

Two days.

Two days is all I have to endure being confined by a damn bicycle chain, to feel degraded and helpless and humiliated and pathetic.

So pathetic.

I am pathetic.

I fucked my mum's husband. I let him do things to me I thought were normal because I saw it in porn. I watched videos, wanting to see someone loving, wanting to see something that might tell me it wasn't okay for him to just keep bending me over and shoving himself so far inside of me that I could feel him prodding, barging my insides, hurting me until he came, until I stopped bothering to beg for it to end anymore.

Sex education opened my eyes.

Sex education told me that those movies... they weren't a clear representation.

But for now, I have to accept them as a reality.

I have to accept this as my reality.

I have to make him think I love him. Make him think I appreciate all that he's done, that confining me and making me piss myself is for my own benefit.

Because that's what his deluded mind believes.

I have to make him think I'm safe to wander around this new house, that those shutters will confine me, make him think it's okay.

He told me the other day, during one of his nightly rambles, where he just sits and talks at me as if his sick words are something profound, that comfort is the most helpful characteristic of human beings.

"Comfort breeds complacency, complacency breeds lethargy,"
he told me. That the, "Oh I'm just out for ten minutes I don't need to close the windows," attitude is what prompts him to say, "Oh my, they have no idea what I can do in ten minutes."

But I do.

I know exactly what he can do in ten minutes.

He can strip me down from my waist, plunge himself into me like he was plunging a stingy shit down a toilet, and fuck me until I cry and convince myself it's normal.

I have to remind myself it's not.

I have to keep some humility.

Someday this will be a story I tell, an anecdote I share.

Someday this will be a memory of a time when I became triumphant.

Someday, someday, someday...

Someday will never come.

I have to believe it will.

I have to convince myself there is a purpose to my suffering, that watching my mum die and watching Mark get hacked to pieces and watching him think he's doing this all for me; I have to believe that all of this, all of it, will eventually mould into something tangible, something I can use to divert his attention.

I have to believe in fight or flight. Either I take an opportunity to run, the right opportunity, or I find a knife or an object and bludgeon him to death, stab him until he knows suffering like Mark and my mum did.

Mark...

Oh, god...

I had to watch you...

I had to watch you, Mark, watch you as any hope of life returning left...

I can still see that bloody face, those eyes that dropped the way gravity pushed them, and pretend that they would reignite.

Not anymore.

Because he chopped you up and fed you to the pigs.

It hurts to say it but I have to so I can conquer it, I have to acknowledge what he has done so I can achieve victory over it.

I have to.

I have to... what? What do I have to do?

I have to do nothing.

I have to accept death, welcome it like an enemy I have made amends with.

I have to pretend there's a god, so I can pretend I will be reunited with mum.

But there is no god.

There is nothing omnipotent and powerful that would allow this to be.

So I have to be patient and wait for him to fall into his own trap.

Comfort.

Complacency.

Lethargy.

Even if it takes days, weeks, months, even years – these are the signs I look for. The signs I await. The characteristics he craves in others just as I do in him.

So I will accept him fucking me, and I will pretend to love it like he thinks I do.

So I will come to terms with his treatment of my mother, pretend he did it for us, pretend even though my insides twist and my throat lurches and my mind screams a million migraines – I must pretend.

I can let it all go afterwards. I can confront it then.

For now, I will appreciate it.

I will say thank you.

Thank you for murder.

Thank you for my torture.

Thank you for showing me how much I love you.

He doesn't even love me, though, does he? He's just infatuated. Obsession. It's vulgar jealousy that I had Mark and he did not like it. He fucks my mum and he fucks his whores and he pretends that it's okay, but my indiscretions are exactly that – indiscretions. Acts of malice.

And I have to pretend that that's okay.

That that's how it is.

I have to love him.

I have to appreciate him.

I have to want him.

Because that is how I escape. By creating the right moment that I can make my move.

So I am patient.

And I await his return.

And I will pounce on him and ride him until he thinks I've seen the light.

I have to, after all.

As it is the only way I am going to survive.

28

THE TWO DAYS pass in peace. I only see Flora on the occasion I bring her food and empty the bucket I generously donated to her. My decision to remain unspoken during our brief interludes is a tough one, but I feel I have done enough pampering toward her.

She needs to reciprocate.

Reciprocate, or there is no need for me to bring her to this house and give her the freedom to wander.

Reciprocate, or there is no longer a need for her to remain in my life, or in hers.

So, on Friday, I allow the movers to come into the house and collect the few bits of furniture I will keep. Honestly, any items I take are going to be put in one of the many, many rooms I will probably never enter or even wander through. There are seven floors with more rooms than I can count, and I just want them filled. All the rooms that mean anything will be getting brand new furnishings.

Flora remains silent as the removal men work. She seems to have stopped her screaming and protesting. I don't know if this is the surrender of hope on her part, or hope that I will resume my attention toward her.

Honestly, if a man is willing to remove your buckets of excrement and still fuck you, you should jump at the opportunity.

So, once Friday has been and gone and the evening has arrived, and the new house is ready, and it is time vacate this abode that seems miniscule in comparison, I saunter to the basement, and I pause.

I wonder what state I will find her in.

I wonder if she knows that this next interaction will determine her fate.

I open the door slowly, allowing my silhouette to cast a shadow over the steps. I pause, wanting her to know this is different. This is not the routine of food delivery or wastage removal. This is the final test, the moment that means something. The time when the silence ends.

My hands remain in my pockets and I take my time inquisitively descending into the basement. It is cold in here, and there is such little light. It is the kind of conditions that brings out who one truly is. Either you cave and you mellow into submission, or you stand up and embrace your realisations.

Let's see which it is.

I stand at the bottom of the steps and watch her. I do not advance, do not move, just stand, and see what she does.

She rises to her knees. She looks like she's been crying, but she at least stops it for me. She looks different. No pitying herself, none at all – she is propped up, leaning toward me hopefully. Her face looks weak, but a different kind of weak – a sad weak, rather than a resentful one.

It is the look of change.

She is like a pet, greeting its owner eagerly as they return home.

One of her hands strays from her body, reaches toward me, as if to grasp at me, but to find I am not in reach.

"Gerry..." she says, and I hate it when she calls me that, but this time it's okay. It feels comforting, almost. Like a warm embrace.

She reaches out for me again and I step forward, just enough that her fingers can scrape my belt.

"I'm sorry..." she whimpers, her voice a whisper, her body hunched in distraught apprehension. "I'm so sorry... you were right... I should be grateful... so grateful..."

This could, of course, all be a trick. I am not good at reading people and lies often pass me by; hence why I hate deceit in a person. It is a deplorable characteristic, and I would wish a fate of immortal death upon the wretched being who would dare enter into a deceitful exchange.

But this feels different.

I am hopeful in a way I have not been since I placed her mother's head in the sink and watched her drown.

"Please, come back to me," she begs. She is on her knees looking up at me and one hand is stroking hopefully down my chest and the other is resting gently on my erection. A naïve person would be fooled into thinking this is an unknowing placement of the hand.

I know better.

"You were so right, and I couldn't see it. You did all this for me and I have been so, so ungrateful. Please take me to our new house, please let us start our true lives together, one where we can share a bed and a home and a..."

A glint in her eye changes the mood. She can see the arousal in my face, I know it, and her hand presses firmer on my penis and fuck it's been too long.

"I want you," she tells me, a sexy whisper, husky and full of craving. "I want you like I had you before."

She sits down and spreads her legs. Her skirt rides up to the top of her thigh and I know what's under it.

"Just like you like it."

She turns over and she lifts her backside into the air. She is unclean and with days old urine stains on her shins and she stinks abominably – but I am too fucking horny to give a shit.

She even lifts her hair up, ready for me to grab it, which I do, and she gasps, excited, ready for me.

I slide her underwear down and it's tiny and it stinks and I touch her. She's already wet. I slide right in and she grunts with a feminine pout on each masculine thrust.

I go harder and harder and she grunts for me, grunts in a way she never used to, and maybe this whole ordeal has changed her, maybe she does feel differently, maybe she has had an epiphany and she realises how much she likes being treated like a dirty little whore, so I treat her like one, and I grab her hair harder and it only makes her scream more and more and more and I turn her over.

For the first time, I want to see her face as she cums.

I fuck her harder and harder and I put my hand around her throat and at first she is hesitant, she thinks I'm going to hurt her, but I'm not really, it's just for show, and she smiles this smile with a sexy half slant and I go in deeper and deeper still until I can't contain myself anymore and I explode inside of her, grabbing her hair and yanking her head back as I do and she does.

She screams, but in the way I want her to scream.

And it finishes.

And I lie there.

And I look at her.

Her eyes seem bigger somehow. Her face is spacious.

She leans up and she kisses me on the lips. Softly. Like this is something romantic, and she sees that I don't want that, and she pulls away.

"Is this okay?" she asks.

I shrug.

"Sure," I say, feeling better about it now she's asked.

She kisses me again and I don't kiss back, but at least it makes her happy. If that's what she wants.

Her mother was the same.

Always wanting to kiss me in that moment after where you both remain still and reflect on what you've just done. But, unlike her mother, she doesn't insist on talking. She allows the moment to just be, and we share it together, until I know all of my dick has emptied into her and I pull it out and I stand and I do up my belt.

I look down at her.

She looks up at me.

"I'll get you some clothes."

"Please can you get my flowery dress," she says. "I know you like me in my flowery dress."

Fuck.

What a change.

This is the version of Flora I can deal with.

Always wanting to appease me.

I rush upstairs, fetch her dress, and she takes it, then asks if she can have a shower first. I allow it, and then we get in my car, her flowery dress perfectly outlining her body that is not such a pubescent body anymore. She has curves that accentuate her slim outline now. She has breasts, albeit small, petite ones – but I wouldn't want them any bigger.

She places her hand on mine as I put the car in gear.

Then she retracts it and looks out the window.

"Is it far?" she asks. "I am so excited to see it."

You'll love it, Flora.

You'll just love it.

It's a modern classic, just like you.

Just like my Flora.

29

THE NEXT FEW days pass by like a dream; one of those dreams you are positive is real but just can't be, as the dream is too damn good.

Flora loves the new house. She says it and I can see it in her face, the awe with which she looks around, the way she marvels at the architecture and the magnificence of the modern interior of downstairs and the classic interior of upstairs, the way that the coffee maker just dispenses her coffee and the wine she can help herself to in the fridge.

And not just any wine, either. Not the prosecco she'd get for a few quid from a supermarket or the own-brand value wine Lisa used to stock in the fridge. I'm talking real wine. I'm talking less Thunderbird Classic Pinot Grigio, I'm talking more Domaine Leroy Musigny Grand Cru imported especially from Burgundy. Less Rose Zinfandel, more J.S. Terrantz Maderia, made in Portugal in the exact same year Thomas Jefferson began his second term.

Not that I give a fuck about Thomas Jefferson, I just want to highlight to you how old this wine is.

And some people say a wine ageing doesn't actually make any difference.

I would say that those people don't have the money to buy properly aged wine.

On Saturday we fuck in the kitchen over the counter, she screams with manic pleasure on every thrust, and she begs me to cum and I politely oblige her.

On Sunday we stain the sofa in the living room and I have it replaced almost instantly afterwards. I look down at her as I fuck her in missionary – yes, missionary, but not boring missionary as I strangle her and it makes her cum even harder.

And on Monday my dick aches as we fuck in the hallway and the bathroom and on the first set of stairs. The stairs I enjoy in particular as my thrusts are so impressive that we start on the bottom step and end on the top.

She begs me for more but I have to let my dick rest. It's aching too much to even piss at this point, and I love how rampant, how enthusiastic she has become.

Honestly, it makes me wish I'd killed her mother sooner.

If this is the life we can live...

We never make a meal. We order the best takeaway and, on Monday evening, I even grace her with a meal out. She offers to cook for me to say thank you for everything, but I decline – she will never have to cook again. Not with me.

That is not the life I will subject her to.

No more fortitude, no more prison service, no more repressed embellished femininity. She can unleash her womanly side and then I can fuck that side then we can eat the most expensive food and throw away the leftovers.

We go to Carluccio's on the Monday evening – although, it is no longer Carluccio's. It has already been taken over by someone else and the name has changed. The same waiters and waitresses, just no fat prick coming out and saying hello.

Yes, I know I said I liked him, but that was until he almost ruined the homage I had presented to Lisa. There was a right time to reveal the truth, and it was now, not then, and he deserves to be pig's shit.

We both order the squid to start and go onto the roasted pork belly to finish. I insist she tries the crème brûlée for dessert and I have the profiteroles. She gets custard on her nose and I wipe it off and she giggles, and I see those freckles again.

When we are back on Monday, we sit on the sofa and watch television. I don't usually like to subject myself to menial flashing images, but we are both so knackered there is nothing else to do.

She moves toward me and places her head in the curve of my armpit. I don't like to cuddle, but I allow it as a reward for how much better company she has been recently. She moans as I put an arm around her and squeeze, but a nice moan, a moan of *oh this is really wonderful.*

And then the local news comes on.

"Police are still hunting for the missing teenager who did not return home from school. It has been almost ten days since Mark Cunningham was last seen, and police are appealing for anyone who may have knowledge of his whereabouts."

They cut to a press conference with a woman and a man sat behind a desk. The man has his arm around the woman who sobs into a teddy bear. Weird, as Mark was way too old for a teddy bear.

Maybe it was from when he was a little kid.

Or maybe he was just some fucking nutjob who still played with teddies.

"If you see Mark," says the man, trying to be plain-faced and stern, more so than the weeping woman anyway. "Please, please, let the police know. We miss him so much, and we are desperate to have him back."

A journalist in the audience puts his hand up and asks, "If Mark is being held against his will, what message would you have for his captor?"

The woman looks deep into the camera, as if her eyes are looking at me, piercing into me.

"Please talk to him," she says, breaking the stream of tears for just one moment. "Mark is a kind, gentle boy. Mark would never hurt anyone, and if you just spoke to Mark, just had a conversation, you would see that. And you would see that Mark does not deserve to be hurt."

I know what she's doing.

She's using Mark's name again and again as if to try to humanise him. To make his captor see him as a human.

He was a means to an end, you red-faced wretch.

And he's already dead.

I scoff, unintentionally, at the thought. Here she is desperately appealing, no idea that her boy's body has already been digested in a farm pig's gut.

"He was last seen outside his school," says the news reader, with the image now cutting to an aerial shot of the school, then cutting to CCTV of him walking away. "This is him walking away from his school, the last image before he disappeared."

I look at Flora, realising that she has said nothing throughout this entire report. She wasn't that receptive to the sight of Mark in the boot, and I wonder if this may shatter the impenetrable pleasure that we have created for ourselves.

I peer downwards, in an attempt to see her face.

She doesn't look back at me.

Her face is an empty enigma.

Whatever she's thinking, she is keeping it to herself.

I turn the television off.

I remove her from the curve of my armpit, where her head was starting to get a bit heavy anyway, and I look at her.

She doesn't look back at me.

And this better not ruin it.

Everything is so perfect, everything is excellent, and if she dares let a little news report shatter the new life we have created for ourselves, I swear, I will gut her right here and now.

"Look at me," I say.

She doesn't.

I grab her chin and turn her face toward me.

"Why didn't you look at me?"

She doesn't say anything. Then she does. She smiles and puts her hand gently on my wrist, which allows me to release the tight grip I have of her.

"I'm sorry," she says, her voice so springy and kind. If honey could talk, it would sound like her.

"Are you still mad at me for Mark?" I ask.

She thinks about this, which at first annoys me, then I realise it's good that she thinks about it. I want a real answer, an answer that will be genuine, not a forced, immediate reaction that would probably be a lie.

"No," she says. "I understand you need to do things like that."

"Like what?"

She shrugs. "Killing people. You need to do it. And that's okay."

She's right.

And as soon as I realise it, the burning itch returns.

I *need* to do it.

And, suddenly, I need to do it again.

I look at Flora's throat. So delicate, so dainty. The human body is so easily wounded. You'd have thought the dominant species would be less easy to harm, but just a squeeze of that throat for a minute or so and that indestructible mass of skin and blood would be a vacant mess.

I don't want Flora to be the one, though. I want to keep her around. Our lives together are just too marvellous, too wonderful.

Maybe I'll go out.

Before I've even considered it, the decision has been made.

I will go out.

I will quench my thirst and I will return, fully recharged and ready to continue our life of ecstasy.

"What is it?" she asks.

"I'm going to go out for a bit," I tell her. "I won't be long."

"Okay."

"I will leave the shutters down."

"Don't you trust me?"

What?

Don't I trust you?

I can't imagine the last few days not being pleasurable for her too, and maybe I should trust her.

But not yet.

Not because she asked.

But because it feels right that she should be left unguarded.

"In time," I tell her.

I go to stand, and she stands and she grabs me and she pulls me close and she kisses me with a wide, aggressive mouth, waving her tongue around mine, and grabs my dick in one hand as she does it and I am so hard, so fucking hard.

Then she pulls away.

"Come back soon," she tells me, and gives me that kinky little smile she has.

I put the shutters down and I go to my car and I leave. Never mind that we have already fucked three times today – she has aroused me once more, and I feel fierce, and ready to fuck again.

But I will kill instead.

Honestly, you should try it. The thrills are almost the same. The pleasure of fucking and the pleasure of killing are like they are entwined, gracefully melded into the same set of senses, where you cannot have one kind of pleasure without the other.

And I am ready to quell the urge.

I am so, so ready.

I COULD

I COULD WATCH him leave from the window, but there is no window I can see out of. I would not even know what time of day it was if it weren't for the 10 o'clock news.

As soon as he leaves, I rush from room to room, searching for a window without a shutter. There are so many rooms it takes me more than half an hour to leap from one to another, a frantic panting the soundtrack to my desperation.

There is no break in the fortress.

No way out.

There are no cracks in the walls, no weakness in the foundation, nothing.

I truly am going to have to earn his trust.

Let him feel so secure that he eventually allows me to wander in a house not bound by shutters.

I could take a knife. Surprise him when he returns. Pounce on him and dig it into his neck.

But there is too much risk.

I could fail to take him by surprise.

I could fail to put the knife in hard enough.

I could lose all the trust I have already gained.

I know I have no choice. The only way is to keep going, to keep letting him fuck me, to keep letting him degrade me and keep pretending that I love it.

Three times in one day I have had to do this.

I have had to scream like he wants me to, at the moments he wants me to, and beg him for more, just like he wants me to.

I could stay numb. I could keep thinking it's only temporary.

I could also be here forever.

And then it dawns on me.

A thought that is all the more poisonous than the hundreds of thoughts constantly battering against my skull like drunk scorpions flushing out all hope...

Someone's going to die tonight.

He needs to kill. He itches for it. He fucks me instead, but it's never enough. He desires it, probably even more than he seems to desire me.

I could call the police.

I could see if there is a working phone.

I could end up being recorded, or it could only dial him, or he could be alerted to a 999 call in some way.

I could just accept it.

And that is the most awful thought, the realisation that I am just going to have to live with the knowledge that, right now, someone innocent, like my Mark, like my mum, is losing their life.

I fall to my knees and I cry.

I must cry.

I have to get it all out now, I have to release the emotions and the torment and the hurt and the pain and–

What if he has cameras?

What if he sees me cry?

I don't think there are cameras, but...

I could be caught.

And I can't make any presumptions.

Even when he's not here the façade has to continue.

I hate him.

I hate him so, so much.

I could wait until he's asleep and he's next to me and take that opportunity to kill him.

I could also fail.

I can't just be hasty, I have to wait, have to see it through. Have to pretend that it was okay that he murdered Mark, that he chopped him up in front of me and fed him to pigs.

I could try to wipe the image from my mind, but it's not in chalk, it's tattooed there – never leaving.

The murder by a man who I tell I love and tell I want and cuddle up to like there is genuine affection.

I could keep kissing the man who murdered my mother.

I could keep screaming with pleasure as the man who drowned my mother in the kitchen sink drives his cock further inside me.

I could ignore the pain, I could pretend I do like it, pretend I even love it, I could convince myself to enhance the performance.

I could live a life full of trauma that I will never recover from.

In fact, I will, I know.

But not until I'm out of here.

Not until I've survived.

All the awful memories, the repeated, forceful fucking, the disgust with myself for letting the man who tortured those I loved even after they died...

I pick up the phone that hangs in the kitchen, a landline attached to the wall. Out of curiosity, I put it to my ear to check for a dial tone.

There is one.

I press a button, and a message begins... "I am sorry, but outward calls are disabled from this device."

I drop it.

I try not to cry.

Please don't cry, Flora, please don't.

I could get caught.

I could undo all that I've had to endure already.

I look up to the heavens, but I only see my wooden prison cell.

I try the shutters again, but I give up on the second one.

There's no point.

I am in here.

Even if I escaped, he'd find me.

I could bide my time.

I could.

I could... because I have no other choice.

How will I even know when the time is right?

I punch the wall. My fist hurts and it reddens but I don't care, I punch it again. It's firm and it's painful but FUCK I need to feel something.

I have turned my feelings off, killed my pride, my awareness, my tears, and I could keep doing that but–

I rush to the bathroom.

The squid lurches up through my throat and lands in the toilet bowl along with bile and blood and wine.

He thinks he's treating me. He thinks he's done this for me. He thinks it's what I want.

I could convince myself of it too, as long as I forget my mum, forget...

I can never forget my mum.

But for now, she needs to be pushed aside.

And I am so sorry I have to neglect you. I am so sorry I have to keep having sex with him, keep letting the hands that took your life rub themselves all over my sixteen-year-old body, to put themselves inside of me and around my neck as his sweaty face heaves over me, as if I would actually be turned on by what he did to you.

Mum, I'm sorry.

I know you'd want me to survive, but not like this.

Not like this.

I could give up.

But I won't.

Because you would not let me.

I could love you, mum, but for now, I can't.

I could love him, and for now, I must.

And it makes me sick again.

So I wait for him to return.

Wait so I can rush up to him and fuck him like he wants me to.

Knowing that I could not survive another day of this.

But knowing that I will.

I could bury you, mum, but I have nothing to bury.

Please don't be disappointed in me.

I could never let a man touch me again after this.

But first, I have to endure.

I could endure.

I could.

But I don't know for how much longer.

Soon, he will return, and he will put the hands he'd used to kill on my breasts, squeezing them, rubbing those hands all over my skin, touching me in every place he shouldn't.

He'll rip my clothes off knowing he will buy me new ones.

And I will forget about you, mum.

Because it's the only way.

I could hate myself forever.

I could love him for now.

And I could not do a single thing to change the mess that I could have avoided had I just said no the first time it ever happened.

So I sit here, and I wait. For the performance to resume. For the trauma to get even worse.

And I could do nothing else, even if I wanted to.

30

I DRIVE through town with my phone connected to Bluetooth. *A Collection – Josh Groban* plays, and he's quite the singer, this chap. I recall watching him in *Ally McBeal,* back when that was big and I would watch Calista Flockhart, caught somewhere between arousal and confusion that someone that thin could actually exist. I hear she married Harrison Ford, and I wonder how he didn't crush her.

I'm already bored. I have barely begun my cruise until I find myself fed up of constantly looking upwards for CCTV. Even if I venture into a domain where CCTV isn't prevalent, my car will be sighted going into that domain.

This necessitates the requirement for me to seek someone out in a dimly lit part of the world where I know I will not be tracked and people will dwell that will not be missed.

This is, of course, the street where you will find the hookers.

Not the hookers I have previously become accustomed to, I might add.

See, there are two varieties of hookers.

There are hookers that prefer to be called *escorts*. They cost hundreds, even thousands, and concentrate less on just the carnal act of fucking, and more on the fantasy with which you wish to involve the carnal act of fucking. When you phone they will ask your requirements, and there will be an element of conversation beforehand. They will be beautiful, but of all beautiful body types. There really is any sort you wish, and they always ensure they are clean every few weeks.

Then there are the *whores.* The ones who hang around the streets, occasionally give money to a pimp or suck their dick for protection as they jack themselves up on heroin, hang around on street corners in fishnets looking fucked to the eyeballs, waiting for some punter to pay them a handful of cash to do something said punter could probably do to themselves with far better execution.

Escorts, you see, would be missed. They would have family, a high-class, lavish lifestyle, and would ensure that someone knows where they are going and with which client at all times.

Whores, no one could care less. If they disappeared off the street, the only person to notice would be the other homeless vagabonds who wouldn't have to compete any more for what they find in their dumpster.

And it is just that type of wench I see at the end of this street.

I park my car and kill the lights. I dislike parking my Mercedes in this street, but I will not be leaving it unattended for long.

I wait to see if there is a pimp attached to this woman, or if there are friends working this street with her.

There is not.

And she can barely stand up straight. She has a cigarette

in one hand that misses her mouth and tinges her face, of which she does not seem to feel.

I hang on for forty-five minutes, watching her having conversations with no one, stumbling around the same spot, and continually hiking her menial leather skirt up every time it rides down her ripped fishnets – and not ripped fishnets in that stylish way some women wear them nowadays; that style really gets me, I like it. They are ripped because they are barely still intact. They look like string around a turkey, pressed against her thighs like barbed wire, her skin bursting through the cracks like Play Doh squeezing through a tube.

Enough waiting.

I step out, look up and down the street, and check that my car is locked three times. She can hear my footsteps from the classy tap of my shoes – that sound made with the most perfect of heels.

She spots me and uses a fence to steady herself. She puts out her cigarette and turns to me and I find smoking deplorable, especially when you can barely afford to eat.

"Hey, honey," she says, slurring, stumbling, her eyes widening then wandering away and closing then opening again.

"Really," I say, "this is rather abysmal, wouldn't you agree?"

"Huh, wassat, honey?"

She looks at me in the way that stupid people do – you know when they've said something they think is really profound but is unimaginably uneducated, and they just stare, wide-eyed, expecting you to engage with them just because you happen to be in the same street or mode of transport.

"You wanting some – some – some..." She can't even get

whatever synonym of sex she wishes to use out of her overblown lips.

My God, I have just noticed her lipstick. It looks like a clown with poor functioning hands has decorated their face. There is just nothing discreet about this woman whatsoever.

"I believe you mean to ask if I would like some sex, or a hand job, or something between, correct?"

She smiles like a clown too, and nods as her eyelids lilt again.

"Well, I would rather incinerate my genitals on a barbeque."

"... huh?"

Another thing I despise: people who grunt instead of saying *pardon* or *excuse me* or even just a simple *what did you say?*

It repulses me.

I take out my knife.

She sees it and I hold it up just at the moment my bloody phone goes.

"Aw shit," I bark, and I take it out.

It's an alert from the house.

It's the phone.

Someone is trying to use the phone.

But who could possibly...

Flora.

Why on earth would she wish to use the phone?

I check, and no call has been made, but a single 9 has been entered.

I deny myself the instinctive thoughts that she could be going against my wishes, betraying my trust, that she is lying to me.

But how could she lie to me?

No one could fake happiness like this, no one could feign the pleasure or the way she tries to cuddle me and...

Is she hurt?

Could she be trying to get to an ambulance?

The hooker still hasn't moved. She's seen my phone and my knife and she still hasn't moved.

I ring home.

I wait.

It rings and it rings and it rings and it rings.

She doesn't answer it.

Is she incapacitated? Is she hurt? Does she need me?

I put my phone away.

"Are you going to–" the hooker begins to ask, but I don't have the time.

I stab her in the gut, in the chest, in the neck, in the face, and again and again in all the places that I have yet to stab. By the time I've finished she's a bloody heap on the ground.

She could survive, of course. But she won't. Because no one will care enough to take her to the hospital.

I don't even need to dispose of the body. No family will report it. My DNA is not on file with the police, there will be no connection between anything on this knife and the blood seeping out of her body.

The only obstacle would be if she was a witness to her own attempted murder.

Just to make sure, I drag the knife across her throat, standing to the side to ensure the blood does not splatter on my suit.

That will do it.

I leave her, choking and wriggling, and by the time I have returned to my car and looked in the wing mirror she is not moving anymore.

It feels good, but it's not as satisfying as I wished it to be.

But I need to make sure Flora is okay.

There could only be two reasons for her dialling a 9 in the phone.

And I do not wish for her to be hurt.

But, I hope for her sake, that she is.

As the other reason can't bare thinking of.

31

I WALK through the door slowly and sternly, particularly, listening – but for what, I'm not entirely sure.

Sobs? Groans of pain? Moans of needing desperate help?

No sound meets me.

I walk further in. There is no broken legged girl at the bottom step, no body bleeding to death in the kitchen as a result of a catastrophic cooking accident, and no girl with slit wrists in the bathroom.

What there is, however, is Flora, sat on the sofa, watching the seventy-two-inch television. She is wearing one of my shirts and nothing else but socks. Her thighs are curved and her legs are smooth and immediately I want to take her, but I control myself.

Just for now, I control myself.

She turns and she smiles at me. An adorable smile. A loving, caring smile.

The smile of someone who is not injured whatsoever.

"Hey, you," she says ever so sweetly. "Did you have a good night?"

I nod.

"Did you do what you need to do?"

She means *did you kill somebody?*

I don't understand why people do this, but they tend to avoid asking questions they aren't comfortable with directly. Another example is, "has he passed on?"

The word is *died.* Use it and make it clear to everyone what you are on about.

I say it again: I hate subtext.

Not just because I can't read it, but because it has no use. People who aren't direct are trying to convince themselves of something more than anyone else.

"Yes," I finally answer. "Yes, I did."

"Are you feeling better for it?"

She is still asking me so sweetly, so adoringly.

Just how I would want her to ask me.

"Are you okay?" I ask, ignoring her question.

"Of course."

"No injuries?"

She sticks out her bottom lip and shakes her head.

"No close call injuries?"

"Not that I can think of."

"No reason to need an ambulance, no reason to call out?"

"Nope."

I take a step toward her, keeping my hands in my pockets, biting my lip and looking around.

"Have you used the telephone?"

She looks at me and I see it. Just a momentary flicker, I see it – the widening of her eyes, the recognition that she has been caught.

Now she's trying to decide – does she make up a lie or does she deny it?

"I did," she finally says.

Ah, the lie it is.

"Why?" I ask, my voice curt and calm.

"I was going to order a pizza," she says. "But I didn't know any numbers and the phone wouldn't dial out."

"And how would you imagine a pizza delivery man would be able to give you a pizza through the shutters?"

She shrugs, then she giggles. "I know, I was quite silly. I completely forgot!"

"And a phone number would normally begin with an area code, which would begin with a zero, would it not?"

I crouch in front of her and I can see up her shirt just I can see through the destructible lie she has concocted.

"Like I said, I didn't know any–"

"But if you went to dial out, you would start with a zero first, would you not?"

She nods, warily.

I put my hands on her shins.

I rub my hands up and down affectionately, feeling her skin – damn it's smooth – feeling her legs as I rub further and further up until I'm rubbing the inside of her thigh.

"I need a verbal answer, if you please."

"Yes," she says, her cute façade beginning to fade. "Yes, it would."

"Then why, oh why, did the number you went to dial begin with a nine?"

"I'm not sure that it did–"

I cease my sensual rubbing of her legs and part them, digging my fingers in, my thumb piercing through the inside of her thigh, squeezing her skin and muscle through the cracks of my fingers, harder and harder until she starts to wince and the tears start to form.

"You are lying to me," I point out.

"Please, I am not, I want to be with you, why would I–"

I grip harder still. She screams out.

"Please, stop!" she begs.

"Then tell me the truth."

"I am!"

"You are not!"

"Please, just stop, please, I love you and I want to be with you and I just want to–"

I can now feel her bone rubbing the edge of my fingers and I can hear her moan even harder and it satisfies me in a way I can never quite articulate.

She reaches out and puts her hands on the side of my face, despite the pain, and she cups my cheeks, and her tearful eyes stare into mine with a distant hurt, a need for me, a yearning for me to trust her.

I take my hands away and she rushes from the sofa to her knees, so she is knelt before me, her body up against mine. She puts her arms around me and squeezes me, and she begs me to forgive her, to listen to her, to just hear how she would never want to hurt me or leave me or betray me again.

"Then explain," I say.

"I just pushed a button," she claims amongst the hysteria. "I just pushed a button as I didn't know any numbers and it must have just happened to be a nine I didn't mean to push anything else I didn't I mean it I mean it please I swear I swear I would never leave you never ever!"

She is kissing my neck and she is kissing my collar bone.

I am inclined to believe her.

Against my better judgement, I believe it is possible that she just happened to press a nine.

After all, she only pressed the one.

It was a moment of stupidity.

A weakness where she abruptly realised she would have no way of receiving a pizza anyway.

And she stopped.

And she has taken off my shirt.

And she is massaging my chest with her tongue and I go to grab her but she lifts her hands delicately against mine.

"Please," she says. "Let me just take care of you."

She guides me onto my back and she continues kissing me all the way down to my belly and she undoes my trousers and she slides them off, taking my throbbing cock in her hand. She winks at me and puts it in her mouth.

I forget about everything.

Forget about any distrust or reason to not believe her.

Forget about any way in which I might be wrong.

She loves me, she said it.

She has learnt.

And she is a good girl.

And it takes minutes until I am exploding and she swallows it like a good girl.

And she doesn't take her lips away until all the mess has gone.

And we go to bed.

And she tries to spoon me, but I'm not the spooning type. She goes back to her side of the bed and she closes her eyes and every now and then, they flutter.

And I am asleep almost straight away.

Drifting from a perfect life that I cannot wait to wake up to.

I KNOW

I KNOW I made a mistake

How long until I make another?

Such a simple mistake, yet one I could not see coming.

I know it happened because of me. I know it did.

How foolish I was.

And regaining his trust and convincing him of the lie was the hardest and easiest thing I ever had to do.

He's been inside of me before, but never have I tasted him, never have I had to swallow the seed of the man who...

I know I should stop saying it so much.

I know he killed my mum, I know I'm numb to it, and I know I keep reminding you but he did it and there is nothing I can do but suck the bastard off.

And now he's asleep next to me.

I lie on my back, fluttering my eyelids, pretending that I can actually get to sleep, pretending that laying here, next to him, I can actually relax enough to settle into my unconscious.

I know this can't last much longer.

I know it has to end.

I can't bring myself to keep it going, I can't tell myself to bide my time anymore as my time is empty. I can't keep touching the man who touched my mother and touched Mark as he killed them with those hands.

Those hands.

Those hands those hands those hands those fucking hands.

They grabbed my hair as he came.

As he shot into...

No.

Mustn't cry.

Mustn't wake him.

If he knows I cry, he knows it's fake.

If I step out of bed to go elsewhere, he may awake, he may follow, and the illusion will be ruined.

I know I can't take much more.

I know that I cannot take another night like this.

I can't take him thrusting inside of me, I can't appease him and quell his worries with anymore inane acts of forced pleasure.

I know you don't pity me.

After all, I had sex with him, didn't I?

And I did it for two years.

Two years.

Two whole years I was fucking him behind my mum's back – so now you say, how could I possibly feel such loss from a mother I betrayed so severely?

I know.

But I was fourteen.

I was a child. My body had not long since begun its development, my mind had yet to mature, my understanding of right and wrong did not exist.

But then again, some people live their whole lives without understanding the existence of right and wrong.

Don't they, Gerry?

I know you think there's no such thing.

And maybe you're right.

But I know just as anyone else does that you do not do that to a girl of fourteen, stepdaughter or not.

I don't remember being given much choice.

But I also don't remember saying no or pushing him away.

Does that mean I gave him consent?

By not denying him at the beginning, through the lack of understanding as to what was happening, does that mean it was okay?

I know I shouldn't blame myself, but I do.

Maybe he wouldn't have killed you, Mum. Maybe if it weren't for his desire to have me like this, then...

Stop it.

I know I shouldn't feel responsible.

I am not responsible.

I know.

But I am.

And I can't take it anymore.

I can't take him and his expensive life he thinks I love.

I can't take him and his greasy fingers and the hairs on his chin and the way he looks at me like I'm in a permanent state of undress.

I can't stand feigning love toward the man who hacked up the pieces of my youth.

So it's going to stop.

I don't care about my survival anymore.

I can't wait any longer.

It's a risk, but I'm going to take it.

I know I won't endure anymore before I break down and the image shatters and the performance loses its momentum.

I know he will kill me if he even suspects, but hey... I would rather be dead than be his bitch any longer.

So it is decided.

Tomorrow, I will seek out my opportunity.

I will take it.

I may survive, I may not.

I know it won't be easy.

But do you know what?

I also know I have no choice.

I cannot be this person anymore.

It's time for me to find the opportune moment and break it and run and face the trauma.

I know I will have to face the trauma.

I know I will never recover.

But right now, I know I do not care.

Surviving is all that matters.

Is all that I am thinking of.

And I know that this thought will see me through to the end, whichever end it may be.

32

It is such bliss to wake in the morning without Lisa prodding me out of the bed, encouraging me to go to a work that never existed.

Here, I can just lay, and allow myself to wake naturally.

No alarm piercing through my slumber, no overzealous wife hesitating to request morning sex, and no shitty little house and shitty little life to have to dread facing.

This is it.

This is the perfect life.

Flora isn't next to me when I awake. But it's okay. I'm sure she is not doing anything else as foolish as trying to alert a pizza delivery boy that I would ultimately have to kill.

Still, I wish to know where she is.

I sit up and rotate, placing the tufts of carpet between my toes. I put on a t-shirt to accompany the boxers I am wearing, and I leave the room.

For a moment, I'm unsure where to go. Even I get lost sometimes, it's such a marvellous, grand house. But I recall and I walk down the corridor to the stairs, of which I have to go down two floors to find the ground floor. As I near the final steps, I can hear sizzling and a radio from the kitchen.

In the kitchen, I find Flora, still wearing that fuck-me-shirt with her fuck-me-legs out, and if I didn't have morning wood, I do now.

"Morning," she says, and smiles at me. She flips some bacon in a frying pan.

"Morning," I reply, sitting on a stool at the kitchen side.

She butters some bread and places the bacon from the frying pan into the bread. She places the sandwich in front of me and kisses me gently on the lips, allowing the kiss to linger just enough to excite me, then pulls away.

I notice that she has no breakfast.

"Are you not eating anything?"

"I already had mine," she says, and gazes at me.

Fair enough, I think, until I look to the sink and see no plate.

She could have washed it up, but no plate is in the drying rack.

She could have put it in the dishwasher, but the dishwasher is still propped open and empty.

Maybe she cleaned up and put the plate away. After all, there is a bottle of bleach behind the sink that I am sure was not there yesterday. I am not even sure where the cleaning products are, but she must have found it.

I put the sandwich to my open mouth then pause.

The surfaces aren't any cleaner.

The sink isn't sparkling.

If she used that bleach, there is no sign of its effect.

Then I go to put the sandwich into my open mouth and pause again.

Oh, Flora.

Please, Flora, no.

I hope you didn't.

I really hope you didn't.

Because this would mean you have been lying to me all along. Not just yesterday, but from the moment we had sex in the basement. The moment you said you had seen sense.

That would mean every touch, every piece of affection, every kiss every suck every fuck, all of it, would be a lie.

And I really don't want it to be a lie.

Because then I wouldn't just have to kill you.

I would have to maim you into something no one will recognise.

"What is it?" she asks, twirling her finger around my hand not holding the bacon sandwich.

I place the bacon sandwich on the plate, and I study her face. She could not appear more disappointed, although she tries to hide it.

"Are you not hungry?" she asks.

Maybe she's put out because I haven't eaten the breakfast she made for me. That could be the reason to her disappointment.

Only one way to find out.

"Take a bite," I tell her.

She smiles widely and sweetly.

"I told you, I already had mine," she says.

"I don't care. I want you to take a bite."

"Why?"

"Because I said so."

"Don't be silly, it's your sandwich, I made it for–"

"Take. A. Fucking. Bite."

She stares at me. She looks scared, tiny pores of sweat open up, a little shake of her arm, an O formed with her mouth.

"Really, I made it for you, I just want–"

"Do it."

"I'm not hungry."

I grab the back of her hair and lift her head back, pulling it close to me so her cheek is against the grease of the bacon and her eyes are staring helplessly up at me.

"Please, stop," she begs, "you're hurting me."

"Why won't you eat it, Flora?"

"I made it for *you*!"

"And what did you put in it, Flora?"

"Bacon!"

"And what else?"

"Butter!"

I slam her head against the kitchen side. It leaves a small imprint of blood that incenses me – I do not wish for this house to be anything but immaculate.

"Tell me the truth," I say.

"Please..."

She's crying now. I don't buy it.

I grab the sandwich and I shove it against her mouth. She shuts her lips tightly and I hold her nose and her mouth opens and I shove the entire damn thing into her deceptive gob, then cover her mouth with my hand.

She can't breathe, such is the size of the sandwich. She looks beyond scared now, her wide eyes are beseeching me with tears, mortifying dread seeping from her eyes like blood from the damned.

"Eat it," I tell her.

She doesn't.

She doesn't even bite.

She just holds it between her teeth, not chewing or eating.

"I said eat it!"

She shakes her head, whimpers, her face scrunched up.

"You pathetic little bitch."

I let go and she runs to the bin and opens the lid and spits every bit of it out. I just stand and watch and she scrapes it out of the cracks of her teeth and her gums then rushes to the sink where she fills her mouth from water straight from the tap, and spits, does this repeatedly, before swallowing another mouthful.

Then she stops. Panting. Helpless.

And she turns.

And she looks at me.

And she knows.

She knows she has been caught.

The lying, deceiving, little fucked up piece of shit.

After everything.

All I have done.

All I have forgiven.

All I have offered, the compromises she never asked for, I just offered.

The trust I endowed on her, the confidence, the stupid belief in her lie about the phone.

And the disgust, that all this time, she was just waiting, waiting for the moment to dispatch me, then offends me by choosing such a ridiculous way as poisoning and leaving the fucking damn bleach out as if to taunt me with her severe stupidity.

Yes, she has fucked me over.

And she knows this now.

She looks at me with dread, the knowledge that she is about to die falling over her, that she has made a so very huge mistake.

Sorry, Flora.

But I can't handle liars.

I can't handle ungrateful little wenches.

And I can't handle the rage that you have caused inside

of me.

And I know, in this moment, just as she does, that she has to die.

And she has to do it in the most painful, invasive of ways imaginable.

33

_____

I DO NOT WANT to dirty the walls of my new house. The architecture was polished immaculately before our arrival, and it's so rare that cleanliness is ever to my standard.

Someday, these walls will hear the screeches and be home to the trophies, but not today.

Today demands a different location.

I tell her to put some clothes on.

At first, she refuses. Then, she sees what little sense that is.

I am allowing her the grace of dignity before she walks the gallows. She is wearing nothing but one of my shirts, and I do not doubt that, once we are in public, this will take from her any self-respect she has left.

I do not allow her to be alone, though.

Not that it makes much difference.

I have explored the contours and orifices of that body many times. I have watched it develop, watched the hips widen to child-bearing hips, watched the breasts mould from nothing to triangles, traced with my finger as the curves of those legs and that chest as turned from a girl to a woman.

And I have a sudden wave of nostalgia come over me.

I know that body so well.

It brings me great sadness to decimate it so. That temple of flesh, that warmth of ecstasy... I knew it when it was smooth before she had to shave it to be smooth.

Every birth mark, every evidence of scars, the odd piece of cellulite... it's been mine for so long.

It's such a shame I am going to have to wreck it.

Like a perfect painting I spent years crafting, only to go and paint over it with many brushes of red.

She pauses, holding a dress in her hands. She is in her underwear. Black panties and black bra. Laced. It exposes her buttocks and, as she stands with her back to me, she must know what effect it has on me.

That is why she has paused like that, of course.

The dress is there in her hands. Blue, fitted top with a short, flowing skirt.

She knows that's one of my favourites, too.

She knows.

"What are you going to do to me?" she asks, not looking at me, only turning her head slightly so the daylight accentuates the expert features of her face.

Damn, she is beautiful.

And when she asks me this, she sounds like the lost little girl I discovered when I first married Lisa.

Terrified and with no male role model in her life to guide her.

I gave her that.

And she threw it back in my face.

"Get dressed," I tell her.

"Are you going to make it quick?" she asks, running the dress through her hands.

I can't help but look at her body, can't help but trace my eyes back up and down it, and she is doing this intentionally, purposefully, because she knows how sexy she is and how it drives me crazy and I am tempted to grab her and throw her on that bed and–

And what?

Why don't I?

Just one final hurrah?

But what if that's the opportunity she's looking for...

The temporary ten to fifteen seconds it takes for me to cum inside of her, where I am vulnerable and exposed and unaware – it is the perfect opportunity she needs to pour that bleach down my throat, or pick a knife and cut me or, or, or... or whatever other sick idea she had as to how to do it.

I mean, bleach.

Fucking bleach.

Even I would grant someone the grace of a good death not caused by bleach.

It's tacky, and it's sickening.

And I hate her.

I want to hate her.

I try to hate her.

But I want her.

So fucking much.

"I love you," she says.

"Get dressed," I growl, and I know I should stay calm and this just lets her know it's working but I can't help it.

"You have made me happy. Really, you–"

I march forward, grab the back of her neck, and drag her across the room until I slam her forehead into the wall and the room shakes briefly in the aftermath.

It would be so easy right now.

Just pull down those panties.

Bend her over.

Take her like I've taken it before.

But she doesn't deserve that part of me.

She's trying to manipulate me.

And I will not allow myself to fuck up like she did.

I put my mouth next to her ear. I speak in a low volume, at a slow place, and enunciate every syllable so she understands me.

"I know exactly what you are doing. Put on the fucking dress or I'll put it on you."

"That would be different, wouldn't it?" she says, her voice changed. "For you to aggressively put my clothes on, instead of taking them off."

I turn her around so she's looking at me and, again, my anger flickers as she spreads her arms against the wall and her chest welcomes me and I want to touch her I want to feel her I want to–

I want to kill her.

And that is the priority.

"What's the matter?" she says. "Can't decide whether to fuck me or kill me?"

She sounds evil now, not vulnerable, not begging, she sounds assertive, dominant, and fuck if it doesn't just turn me on even more.

And she knows it.

She knows it because she drops a hand and brushes it against my stiff cock.

I throw her onto the floor.

"Put on the dress."

"Or what?"

"Put on the dress."

"You'll kill me anyway."

"Put on the dress."

"Make me."

"Put on the *fucking dress!*"

She doesn't put it on.

I go to unleash my anger, but again, it's what she wants.

I underestimated how smart this girl could actually be.

"I don't give a fuck," I tell her. "It's up to you whether you want your body to be found with clothes on, or clothes off. Either way, you have ten seconds."

She looks up at me, shooting me a look I have seen so many times in Lisa.

She stands, puts on the dress, and turns to me.

"Zip me up?" she asks.

Reluctantly, I step forward and zip up the back of the dress.

I am so attracted to her.

But I have to remember.

She betrayed my trust.

She used bleach.

She used it to try to kill me.

"How long?" I ask.

"What?"

"How long have you been lying? How long have you pretended to enjoy the life I've given you?"

She steps forward, looks up at me, and spits every word with her newfound spite.

"Since even before you *murdered* my mother."

I want to strangle her here and now.

I want to gut her and twist the knife and watch as her blood squirts down her leg like she squirts as she fucks.

I want to gouge her eyeballs until she can't see what I do to her, only feel it.

But this response is what she wants.

And I can't let her have it.

I grab her arm and drag her down the stairs and through to the garage where the car awaits.

I shove her in the passenger seat, shut it, lock it, and break the lock off.

I don't wish to damage it but fuck it, I could buy a thousand of these.

But I can only kill her once.

I MADE THE MISTAKE

I MADE THE MISTAKE.

I left the bleach out.

He knows I left the bleach out.

But it's not the first.

My mistakes go back much farther than that.

I made the mistake of having a childish crush on the man that married my mother. Of seeing him through the eyes of a child who was only just beginning to learn what it was like to have a crush.

I made the mistake of blushing when you smiled at me, when you said things that made me feel special, when you put your arm around me after mum had gone to bed.

I said it was okay when you accidentally kissed me, that I wouldn't tell. That we could still have our time together. That there was nothing wrong with it.

I made the mistake of keeping it our little secret.

I had my first period and he had his first touch.

I had the last day of my childhood on the day he had his first day inside of me.

I was too old for my age, said my school.

I had changed my attitude, said my mum.

Leave me the fuck alone, said I.

I made the mistake of not telling anyone there and then.

I made the mistake of saying it was okay, people just wouldn't understand, there was nothing wrong with an age gap, you don't love my mum anyway, the marriage was just for show, it was me, and you stayed with her for me, because it was me you cared for and me you wanted and me that you made feel so very, very, very special.

I made the mistake of believing you.

I grew up because you made me.

I saw it as normal because that's what it was.

To me, it was normal.

It was all I'd ever known.

And, if you grow up being told secrets are normal, this touching is normal, this love is normal, then you will come to believe this secret touching and this secret love is just that – normal.

I made the mistake of being like every other child. Reliant on role models and carers and thinking they were right, that they knew best, that everything should be trusted.

You never did anything wrong, Gerry.

Don't you worry.

It was me. All me.

I am to blame.

I attracted you to me. I wore those school skirts and I didn't cross my legs because I was too young to have anything to hide, and I believed you because I'd watched Disney films and the greatest love is always forbidden and you were charming and you made me feel like I was the only girl in the world.

I made the mistake of letting you touch me.

I made the mistake of not being given a choice.

Porn was my first experience of sex. You were my second.

So how would I know different?

Hundreds of videos of THREE GUYS THREE HOLES and FUCK MY FACE and FUCK MY GF and BOUND AND GAGGED and GANG FUCKED ON MY WEDDING NIGHT taught me that this was what sex was.

You bent me over and you were in control and you held my hands behind my back and I screamed because it's what they did and you seemed to like it so I kept going and I made the mistake of believing that it was all okay.

It was all I knew.

It hurt.

I ached inside as you finished.

I ate crushed up morning-after pill for breakfast because it's what you fed to me in my cereal.

I told mum I loved her while I wondered how anyone could do something like this to someone they loved.

But I did love her, and I did do it.

Because you were my teacher and you taught me to do it.

And I made the mistake of being such a great student.

I hated my friends, hated my school, and most of all I hated the sex education lessons I would always get kicked out of because they told us things that shook what I knew.

They said good sex is about good communication.

They said you wait until you're ready.

They said porn isn't a close representation.

And I asked you to slow down, asked you to do it another way, asked you to be gentle and be slow rather than bending me over and fucking me every day when I obediently ran home from school.

I made the mistake of asking.

I made the mistake of running home.

And I made the mistake of believing you when you said I was worth everything and nothing at the same time.

And most of all...
Yes, most of all...
I made the mistake of leaving the bleach out.
But that isn't the mistake that's killed me.
It's just one of many.

34

I DRIVE and I glance at her sitting like a petulant teenager, her lips resting on her hand and her elbow resting on the window.

I wonder how I am going to do this.

What the best way would be.

We drive away from the city and any great area of population and toward the country lanes. Some of them are single track, some are narrow enough to fit two small cars, and they are all surrounded by fields, occasionally with cows but rarely with people.

This is the perfect place, really.

Away from everyone and everything and *fuck*.

What is a police car doing out here?

I haven't passed another car in fifteen minutes, and there he is in the rear-view mirror.

Flora hasn't noticed yet.

But she will. And she may try to indicate something.

My mind races with possibilities of what to do.

I could pull in and let it past or I could break and ram into it or I could just keep going and try not to look inconspicuous or I could *oh fuck* Flora notices.

She sits upright, her body alert, and I can see the thoughts in her mind, I can see her running through her possibilities just as I did.

She is considering whether she could signal to this car, whether she could do something to attract his attention. I may not read people well – but she has made it all too obvious.

It takes this piss, really.

Why is everything out to get me?

"Don't think about it," I tell her.

She finally looks at me.

She looks tired. Bags under her eyes, her face dropped, her eyes lolling. Maybe she hasn't been getting much sleep.

My mind instinctively wonders why when she's so happy and content, and I have to remind myself it was all lies, and she was probably laying there all night planning my demise, working out where the bleach was and what she could do with it.

"Or what?" she said. I know she's being antagonistic, and I really don't have the time for it.

The police car is still behind me. I make an abrupt left turn, not indicating until the last moment, and carry on down another country road.

And there the car is, turning, and coming down the road.

I could kill the police officer.

I mean, I don't want to. It's a noble job and I respect them.

But, I mean, there's no one around.

Except, if he is following me, chances are he will already have radioed in my licence plate. If he disappears, then I will be the first person they go to.

And if I am dispatching of Flora, the last thing I want is

unwanted attention from police officers about a missing officer.

"You're screwed, aren't you?" Flora says.

I frown.

I am not screwed.

What a preposterous accusation.

I just need to wait until the police car goes their separate way.

Except, they turned where I turned.

Why would they do that unless they were following me?

I reach under my seat and take out a large, curved hunter's knife. I show it to Flora.

"I'm screwed?" I taunt her.

She doesn't flinch.

Has she resigned herself to death so easily?

Or is she clinging to false hope by her fingernails?

I slow down and turn into a pub car park, where I wait.

The police car pulls in too.

So I pull away and resume my journey onto the road and *would you just know it* – there in my rear-view mirror the car appears again.

Now I know they are following me.

But why?

Why are they just trailing me, and with such little subtlety?

Why not just pull me over – why follow me?

Unless they have me as a suspect for a murder and the officer is on their own and they are trailing me as they await backup, biding his time until it is the opportune moment.

Firearm police officers could be readying themselves at this very moment.

Other officers could be being called to the location. It's out in the middle of nowhere, it could take them some time.

This could be it.

This wonderful, lavish lifestyle I have created could be brought to an end just as it has begun.

I shake my head defiantly.

No, it will not.

I place the knife beneath the seat, with the handle at the prime position for my right hand to reach down and grab it.

And, just as I do so, the police car signals with a brief wail of siren that they wish for me to pull over.

I do as I am told.

35

THERE ARE different types of officers.

Not that I have had much opportunity or need to interact with many, I will admit that, and maybe my experience is limited to that of biased television shows, news reports, and acquaintances of acquaintances – but since this is my memoir and it is my opinion that matters, I will regail you with my theories as I see fit.

The majority are people going to work. Doing a nine to five, albeit that may not be the shift they are on – but a nine to five in terms of getting up, going to work, then going home, just like everyone else.

Of course, their work involves higher risk and every day involves receiving abuse of some kind, and working under the strain of budget cuts, or so they keep yapping on about, and I imagine this creates a working environment you would have to tolerate rather than welcome.

But the majority are honest, they go about their business, and they try to do their best job.

Then we get the TV officers.

By this I mean the minority who people base the majority

on, and this minority are normally those that appear on television shows that set out to portray them in either an honest or arrogant light.

And these officers are arrogant. They are part of a gang, and the most powerful gang in the country, and they act as a gang – initiating themselves into the gang with their 'first nicking' and so forth, and then protecting those in the gang with a fierce loyalty.

These are the racists that tarnish the headlines that would otherwise be made by the honest officers.

And these are the ones that turn the public opinion against them.

And I am yet to figure out which officer this one is until he walks out of the car and my judgemental mind decides instantly he is the kind that deserves to die.

He is a young male, possibly early twenties – which is sickening in itself. I refuse to be told what to do by a man a decade younger than me. This boy does not know anything of life, of who he is, of the world he inhabits. How on earth can he give me instructions or dictate consequences to my actions when he is yet to experience a deeper level of understanding of the world?

Albeit, it is a corrupt world where society convinces itself of a great many things – many that I have already covered, such as the belief that right and wrong exists, and that if someone does not go according to what the current society deems appropriate, then they are a monster. Go back 150 years and those monsters would be the norm. You just happen to be conditioned by a world that suddenly changes its mind.

I digress.

This young man swaggers up to my car with a hand on his belt. There is no taser on his belt, but I do see pepper spray and a baton. This is noted.

He chews gum, and he does it with a slight opening of his mouth. The only thing more repulsive than his cocky, youthful demeanour. I despise gum, and I despise having to see its white, thick substance slopped around the inside of someone's mouthful of saliva.

Urgh, I want to kill him.

I wasn't planning to. After all, kill a police officer and every police officer turns on you.

His shirt chunks out due to what he convinces himself is muscle, but we all know is a stab proof vest. A vest that covers his chest and not his arms or his neck or his face or his legs or his balls.

In conclusion, it's a pretty fucking redundant vest then, isn't it?

He halts by my open window and he says nothing.

The handle to my knife rests against the back of my ankle.

He just looks at me, not saying anything, filling the silence with the slopping of his gum.

Fuck I hate this guy.

He looks over at Flora, and I just wait for her to say something, I just wait.

But she doesn't.

"Put your hands where I can see them," he tells me.

I await a please.

After all, there's no reason to remove politeness from the equation.

"Put your hands where I can see them, don't make me ask again."

I do not like being told what to do.

If he politely requested, I would acquiesce.

If he tells me again, I will gut him.

"I said, put your hands–"

"I heard you," I say, and I go to correct his manners, then think against it.

I put my hands on the wheel.

His handcuffs are on the back of his belt.

But he doesn't reach for them.

I await the reason for my detainment, wondering how I could kill him should the situation require it. I have killed, but never have I been in a fight. A scrap with an officer may not be a fight I could win. I can't just down right refuse, I have to be smart about this.

"Your insurance," the officer says, still not looking at me. "When did you last renew it?"

I go to object and I instantly remember.

Dammit!

When I bought the car, I acquired a week's insurance with the sales team that would get me started, and with the commotion of the last week I completely forgot to acquire further car insurance.

What a bloody faff.

I can't help but laugh though.

I lift my head back and cackle, guffaw even, and he looks at me peculiarly.

"Is everything all right?"

And this wakes up Flora.

I imagine she was awaiting my arrest for suspicion of murder, but now it's just a few days of expired insurance and she knows they are not taking me away, not for that, not something so easily fixable and with the penalty of a fine.

And now she leans forward, and she starts wailing.

And I am soon going to be forced to act.

"Please help me, he's going to kill me, he's–"

I reach across a hand and press it against her mouth to muffle her, but the damn bitch bites me, she bites my finger like she's biting a carrot and it fucking hurts, and I automatically retract my hand, the middle finger reddening, and she continues to beseech this prick for help.

"Don't leave me with him please he's going to kill me he killed my mum he killed Mark the boy who's missing he's taking me now please–"

"Okay, okay," the officer says, reaching a hand up to calm her down.

She's crying again.

She's always fucking crying.

"Would you like to step out of the car," he tells me.

I sigh.

He takes a step back, a hand on the reverse of his belt. That's where his baton is, I presume. And he is getting ready for whatever I may do.

I could just hit the accelerator and drive.

But that would be a short-term solution.

He would radio it in, and everyone would know it was this car and my description would be out and they would look at the car registration and would know my name and it would all be blown.

This wonderful life I have just built for myself would be over.

I cannot let that happen, at any cost.

"Not really," I say.

"Step out, now."

With his spare hand he goes for his radio.

I can't let him do that either. I can't let him tell others about this. So far, they know he's just looking at me for insurance, but once he says I'm holding someone hostage that all changes.

"All right," I say, and I step out the car, and as I do, I bring out the hunter's knife.

He begins to talk into his radio, "Backup ne–"

Before he completes the third syllable, I launch myself at him, swiping and screaming, and he just backs up again and again.

He brings out his baton and that means he raises his arm, exposing the side beneath his stab proof vest, and I prove just how useless it is as I dig the blade in.

I lower him onto his back as he whimpers.

I rip the radio from his shoulder and throw it far away.

I take the belt from his waist and do the same.

And it is just then that I realise – Flora is not in the car.

She is running away.

I stand, and I see it on his belt.

I do believe I was mistaken.

There *is* a taser.

36

I'VE NEVER FIRED ANYTHING, so I never knew if I was a good shot.

As luck would have it, I am a hell of a shot.

The taser lands on the back of her calf and she falls to the ground, throbbing under the convulsions of electrical shocks.

I do not know how long it will last, so I must deal with the officer quickly – and, despite having met no other cars along this stretch of road, I cannot take the unlikely risk of prying eyes.

The little dick is pulling himself across the ground by one arm, covering his bleeding side with the other.

He's going for his belt.

I walk over and kick it further away.

I acquire his radio and bring it to him.

I mount him.

Not in the way I would mount Flora.

Actually, it is quite similar – but with different intentions.

I place a knee against either hip and I do not put the knife to his throat.

Oh no, most men do not care about losing their lives.

I reach it behind me and place its tip against something far more precious, with just enough pressure he can feel a slight twinge.

His eyes widen.

Now that is something he does care about losing.

"Do exactly as I say or I'll stick it in and twist. It may survive it, it may not – I wouldn't take the risk."

I put the radio to his mouth.

"Tell them that you have issued a fine and a notice for insurance to be acquired, and that you are turning back."

He stares wide-eyed at me.

"Why don't we practise? Say it now."

"Okay, I, er, I am okay, he's fine, he's just–"

I apply more pressure and he screams.

"You sound too dishevelled." I look at his name badge. "Ian. You sound too stressed. Tell them calmly."

"How am I meant to sound calm when you have your knife in my dick!"

"I'm sure you can find a way. Let's try again, shall we?"

I listen to him bumble over the words as I check on Flora, quite a few paces away. The throbbing is lessening, and she is starting to regain the use of her body.

"Okay, dress rehearsal over. Now for real."

I press down on the button, apply more pressure with the knife so he knows I'm not messing around, and he speaks the words perfectly, just as I requested.

The radio confirms what he has said and asks him to go investigate a report of a brake-in somewhere I don't recognise.

"Say yes," I whisper.

He confirms in his police jargon, and they confirm back, and I go to discard the police radio once again – then I have another idea.

"Tell them that a bunch of youths have just stabbed you."

"What?"

"Do it!"

He does as I say.

"Now tell them you've had enough."

"I've what?"

"Tell them!"

He does it.

"Now tell them that you are going to kill yourself. Tell them that you can't take being an officer anymore."

Surprisingly, he doesn't fight me, and he does what I say.

Oh, the power it gives you to hold the life of a man's dick in your hands.

The person on the other end keeps saying, "Ian, Ian, talk to me," apparently alarmed.

This time, I do discard the radio, and I stand.

Flora has now made it to her knees.

She is limping away.

"Flora!" I shout out.

She ignores me.

"Flora, if you run away, I will kill this officer."

She slows down.

"Just go!" the officer says. "Leave me!"

Oh, what a bloody martyr. Another officer who's watched one too many Hollywood movies.

This isn't Hollywood.

This is no movie.

No work of fiction.

This is my memoir, and it happens as I wish it to.

"Flora, I am not going to wait."

She stops.

She turns.

Looks back.

Looks at me.

Looks at the officer.

The officer tries to mouth *just go,* so I squash his face beneath my foot.

"Come here, Flora."

She doesn't come.

But she doesn't leave either.

She truly has no idea whatsoever what to do.

This is quite an ordeal for her, I imagine. A difficult choice. The folly of the weak – does she allow one to die as she lives, or does she allow them both to die, as they inevitably will do.

"You'll kill him anyway," she says, reading my mind.

I shrug.

"You just have to take that chance," I tell her.

"I hate you. I do. I mean it. I really, really fucking hate you."

I shrug again.

I'm past that point now.

The betrayal has sunk in and I've been pissed off, and now I'm just ready for this to be over.

But there's still a long way to go.

"Why did you have to do this?" she asks, and I really do not understand the question.

Her semantics are way off.

For starters, *have to* implies there was never an element of choice. I make no qualms about it, these actions are as a result of a need, but as all psychiatrists will tell you – we make a *choice* whether to act on a need.

And *this* is a general term to which she needs to be far more specific.

I have done a great many things she could be referring to, and I can't just guess as to the event she is referencing.

"Please," she begs.

I'm really fed up of begging. Why is that everyone's instinct?

I would respect someone a lot more if they had a little fight in them before death, but it seems to be such a rare characteristic.

"I won't say anything. Just let me go."

"You expect me to believe you?"

"No, but you can trust me, you can–"

"We are so far beyond that point now, Flora. Really, we are. And this is futile. Get over here now or I kill this officer."

Ian attempts to leap up and fight me but the pain in his side is too much and he falls back down. It is at this point I realise his arm will no longer move when he tells it to.

Lucky, really, as I was so engrossed in this pointless conversation that I hadn't noticed his attempt at a resurgence.

"You've got everything you wanted," she continues. "You have the house, you're rid of the wife, you've got the money."

"Not everything, Flora. I haven't everything I wanted."

Her faces scrunches and looks really ugly. She ducks her head and waves her hands despairingly.

"Why me? Really, please, why me? Because I was young? Because I was easy? Because I was special?"

"Special?" I have a little chuckle. "Oh, Flora, you weren't special. It was just because you were there."

She looks to the officer.

She hesitates again.

But I am not waiting any longer.

I don't want to leave any more blood than I need to.

I take the pepper spray from his belt with his own hand, wrapping his useless fist around it, avoiding leaving any of my own prints.

I mount him again.

And Flora watches as I force the entire bottle down Ian's throat then cover his mouth.

You may think, hey, it's just pepper spray.

But as I watch him empty his mouth of the substance and ingest it down his throat, I can tell you that it is not.

Dependent upon the manufacturer, it also contains cleaning fluid, possibly paint, possibly grease strippers, and propellants such as dymel or nitrogen.

And if you want to know whether or not they can definitely kill you, I can tell you from the sight of the dead man beneath me that, with upmost certainty – yes, it bloody well can.

I WHISPER

I whisper, "What have you done?"

I cover my mouth in shock as my only salvation dies.

As a living man before me fades.

As the person who is supposed to protect me from men like this dies on his own defence.

I whisper, "Oh, God, no..."

Gerald talks, but I don't listen.

He says something about faking suicide.

He puts him in the police car and puts the pepper spray in his hand and props him up.

He takes the handbrake off and turns the steering wheel and closes the door and lets the car fall into a field. It gathers a little speed before stopping at a hedge.

And another dead person is there because of him.

Because of me.

Because I did nothing.

I could have warned him sooner.

But I didn't. I just assumed they were there to help me... Not that they were there about insurance...

Insurance!

Another moment of stupidity, and all I can do is whisper.

I whisper, "You idiot," and I say it to myself, not to him.

He just faked a young officer's suicide.

Surely, they would question the stab wound... Surely, they would question why he suddenly...

I whisper, "So silly."

Have I not learnt anything yet?

Gerald has money that can buy his freedom.

Even if they do question that stab wound, if they do speak to the last person he spoke to by tracking the license plate – there is no evidence he gave that stab wound.

The officer said he was attacked by youths. He said it in the radio.

Even if they did accuse Gerald...

There would be nothing to go on.

His lawyers would probably stop there even being a trial.

No matter what happens, he walks free.

He kills my mum, kills Mark, kills this innocent man...

And he walks free.

That is how he does it.

And I see him thinking it. I see him holding the knife, twirling it, wondering how to get rid of it. He'll have to burn his clothes too, ensure there is none of the officer's blood.

But I know.

I am a witness.

And surely, after an officer claiming he was going to kill himself, police would be on the way.

I just have to stall.

I just have to wait.

I am the key to putting him away, and I whisper it to myself just so I can hear it aloud: "I am the key."

Before he can deal with the weapon and the clothes, he has one more thing to deal with.

Me.

I back away.

He tells me to come here.

But I don't.

I hear sirens.

I hear them coming.

I whisper, "Hurry."

I do not wait for him to get any closer.

I turn.

And I run.

He doesn't come after me.

He gets back into his car and he turns it around and he races after me.

I throw myself over a bush and into a field.

I run and I don't look back.

I sprint and I sprint and I sprint as hard as I can, until I may pass out, until the wobbling the taser has sent through my legs destroys my balance and I fall into a pile of mud.

I go over a fence into another field, through a set of trees and out into another field.

I leap over a fence, fall to my feet, and land on my back.

I get up.

I look over my shoulder.

I look and I search for him.

The sirens are louder.

And I whisper, "He's gone."

I don't see his car, I don't see him, and I might just be safe.

I whisper, "I can't be."

So many nights wondering when I can die, safety just can't seem possible.

But I see the police cars arrive.

I see them, in the distance. Too far away to even hear me scream. I am so many fields away now, so far have I run, but the police are there, they are there, if I can just get to them, I'll be safe.

I whisper, "I'll be safe."

So, I run again.

I stumble all the way across the first field. I feel my legs ache and they feel as if they are wading through water, but this is it, the final push, the final bit of resistance.

If I get through this, I live.

If I get through this, I am safe.

It takes longer than I can guess to get back through the trees as I have lost all sense of time, but it feels far longer than it did when I ran through them.

All the time I search for him – search so I can keep distance between us.

For his car.

For that voice or those steps or that incessant appetite for murder.

The sun is dimming now.

It is getting lower.

I run and I run.

I slow down.

Fatigue takes its grip on me. I push myself through it, but I fall after almost every step.

All the stress and anxiety and despair and repressed grief I have pent up pushes me down, and it feels like roots are coming through the mud and grabbing hold of my ankles and fixing me in place, desperately claiming me, telling me I belong here.

But I don't.

I whisper, "I don't."

And I push forward.

It's raining now.

The perfect cure for evidence.

But when they look for my evidence, they will search for places the rain can't get to.

They will find pieces of him there.

And he will go away to prison, and he will go there for a long, long time.

A few more are in the field now.

I can see them.

Police tape around the car.

Paramedics are leaving, but the police remain.

He must be dead.

But I am not.

I whisper, "I am not."

And I endure the last few moments of agony and I force myself forward.

I can't run any longer.

No more running.

I walk, I wade, I even crawl.

But I make it into the field.

And I can see them, a few football pitches away.

They are still so far away, still across a large patch of grass. I am barely visible to them, but they are all I see.

My salvation.

I whisper, "Help me."

I mean to shout it, but I whisper it.

It doesn't matter.

I will stride up to them and fall into their arms.

I'm free.

Free of him, free of death, free of everything.

Time to face the trauma.

Time to tell my story.

Time to whisper no more.

I take my first step into the field.

And then I see him.

Gerald has changed his clothes.

Gerald stands there, telling them how he was the last person Officer Ian Darling spoke to.

Gerald gives his statement, that he drove away, saw the car veer off, then turned back and called the police straight away.

Some youths ran away, and he was positive he saw some knives on them.

And how he saw Officer Ian Darling swallow something in his car...

Gerald asks if Officer Ian Darling is okay, and the Inspector breaks the news to him. Gerald looks down and covers his eyes and, as he looks up, his eyes pry across the field, and they meet mine.

And they are the only eyes that see me.

How did he change his clothes?

How did he discard the weapon?

How did he act so convincingly?

He smiles. His fingers give a little wave only I see.

I whisper, "Please, no."

And my voice is so hoarse that my scream does not come out.

37

————

IT'S ALL SO EASY.

I thought getting away with murder was supposed to be tough.

Honestly, it's all just so simple.

You give the police a story that fits with the story the officer gave them.

Because, of course, how could I know what he had told them on the radio?

How could I possibly interlink the stories so clearly without knowing?

The answer they come to is that *it's because he's telling the truth.*

There is no blood on my clothes because I have a spare suit in the boot where I also have a safe that I can hide the weapon with the spare tire. With no grounds to disbelieve me there is no reason to look.

And the clothes with little Ian's blood on them are burnt on the fiery carcasses of a farm I passed. A wonderful, convenient opportunity. So much so it could be like I'm making it all up.

But remember, dear voyeur, this is a memoir – there is no lie to anything I am saying.

But that's what happens when you're rich.

All the luck points your way.

The officer thanks me for the statement, takes my details in case they need any more information; though they say my account is so thorough they may only need to ask a few follow-up questions – this officer had only just returned from a period of illness due to mental health issues, another piece of fine luck.

The officer was attacked. The officer killed himself. And there is only a single witness to corroborate the story, and the officer's words in the microphone I couldn't possibly have known about.

I'm sure there will more enquiries, I am sure they will question this further – but I am confident I have covered everything.

I turn to leave.

And, just as I think I am already the luckiest man in the world – I get just that bit luckier.

There she is.

I see her.

And I lock eyes with her.

She could come screaming toward us, claiming I killed the cop and that I abducted her.

But she doesn't.

Because she knows I am too powerful and too indestructible to have fortune not end up in my favour and she will end up just as fucked, back in my possession.

Instead, she freezes, hidden by the shadows of trees. Officers don't think to look, but I am always looking, and I see you, Flora, I see you.

I return to my car and I turn the ignition and it's time to collect what is mine.

It's time to resume our task, Flora.

The police couldn't stop me.

Do you really think you can?

I cackle all the way across the road that loops to the field she is in. She turns and runs away but I bring my car to a stop next to a gate to the field and I leap out and I am so much faster than you, Flora, I am so much faster. You are so tired, so fatigued. You have had no sleep, but I, Flora, have slept the best sleep I've had in a while.

Honestly, if you really wanted to kill me you should have done it while I slept.

But you didn't want to take the risk, did you?

And bleach is what you come up with?

I'm too rich to be fucked over, Flora.

Money gives me luck you cannot afford.

It takes seconds for me to have covered the stretch of the field and to have her back in my arms. She tries to kick and tries to put up a fight but her body is losing energy and losing hope.

We fall to our knees and it annoys me that I have mud on my suit trousers, but soon I will have blood on it too, so I suppose I just have to come to terms with it.

I shush her.

I stroke her hair.

I tell her it's all okay.

She cries again. But these are real tears, ferocious tears, despairing tears.

You thought you got away from me, didn't you, Flora?

You thought the police could save you?

But you are poor. Poor people don't have luck.

I have luck.

I am too fucking rich to be destroyed by some childish little brat.

I enjoyed fucking you, Flora.

Really, I did.

And I enjoyed those few days where I believed you were enjoying fucking me too.

But it's over.

And it's time for it to end.

I take her by the hand, and she doesn't fight, and I drag her back to the car.

She is despondent, but resolute.

She knows her chance to run has gone.

We reach the car.

We stop outside of it.

You lean against it, out of energy, out of fight.

You look up at me, those puppy-dog eyes again.

"Please," you say, in a whisper, because your voice can't produce anything bigger anymore, your body is too empty to make a real sound. "Please, just make it quick."

I smile and I lean in and I lock eyes with you and I say, "Not a chance, Flora. Not a chance."

And I duck your head under the bonnet and I move you into the passenger seat.

And we drive away into the sunset.

38

———

IT'S GETTING DARK NOW, dear voyeur, and I am growing tired of Flora's company. It has been a long day, and I am hungry, and I need the toilet.

Flora is slumped down in her seat, arms by her side, staring catatonically forward, awaiting her death.

This drive is her walk to the gallows.

Oh, I wonder what it is like to know you are about to die a slow, painful, violating death.

Maybe she'll convince herself heaven exists in an attempt to make it all better.

But it doesn't exist, dear voyeur, it doesn't exist.

And even if it did, there is no place in it for a delinquent child who fucks her dead mother's husband.

Not that I believe such a thing is right or wrong, but religion always seems fixed in the black and white view of things.

Then again, the bible does condone abominable acts.

Oh, you don't believe me? You think your religion is all full of love and hope?

Or is it that you choose to ignore those passages that don't fit with your society's conditioning?

Well, let's take a closer look...

If a man happens to meet a virgin who is not pledged to be married and rapes her and they are discovered, he shall pay her father fifty shekels of silver. He must marry the young woman, for he has violated her. He can never divorce her as long as he lives – Deuteronomy 22:28-29.

Not enough?

Kill every man in the town. But they may keep for yourselves all the women, children, livestock, and other plunder. You may enjoy the spoils of your enemies – Deuteronomy 20:10-14.

One more for luck?

When a man sells his daughter as a slave, she will not be freed at the end of six years as the men are. If she does not please the man who bought her, he may allow her to be brought back again – Exodus 21:7-11.

See?

I, society's outcast atheist, is more of a Christian than you are.

At least I learnt about what I hate, whilst you plead ignorance about what you love.

I drive for almost an hour, enjoying the peaceful lull. I do not drive anywhere in particular, I just drive farther and farther into the countryside, until we are so deep in there is not another soul for miles around.

I bring the car to a stop by a field.

We say nothing for a few minutes.

She doesn't move.

I kill the engine.

"Is there anything you wish to say before this happens?" I ask.

She still doesn't move.

"No begging? No pleading for me to take you back? No

desperation for forgiveness, for me to free you and for us to return to the life we had just started to make for ourselves?"

She turns to me, her head slowly rotating, and fixes her angry, evil eyes on mine.

"I would rather die than return to that life."

Ah, and so you will.

And so it is like this that you depart this world.

A defiant little schoolgirl.

A childish little wretch.

A motherless, pathetic, scrawny little sack of unloved skin and bones.

I open the car door.

I return to the boot and seek out my safe. From it I bring out my knife.

I twist the blade, inspecting a few splashes of dried blood. I consider how I will do it. Whether I will stick it in her gut and twist, or whether I will begin by chopping something off just to get started.

I return to the passenger side and open it.

"Get out," I tell her.

She does as she is told, and she walks into the field without my having to say anything.

She just walks, stumbling from one foot to the other, edging along the grass.

I follow her.

Intrigued as to where she wants to die.

She reaches the other side of the field and stops beneath the shadow of a tree. There, she turns to me and looks.

I stop, a few paces away.

And we look at each other.

Two souls, hurting, in pain from the other.

And then she puts her hands at the base of her dress, that

blue dress I picked out for her. It seems weeks ago now, but really it was just this morning.

She lifts the dress over her head and puts it to the side.

And there she stands, her black laced underwear covering the only non-concealed skin of her body.

She is just as beautiful as she has ever been.

She has a body most men would kill to touch.

And it was my body for so long. I witnessed her body turn into this body, I watched the curves develop and the breasts grow and the body hair that she removes on almost a daily basis.

And now I look at it and am overcome with a wave of sadness.

I am going to miss this body.

"Do you want to touch me?" she asks.

Yes.

God, yes.

I want to run my hands all over it, then my tongue, and then grab all the bits that you have kept covered.

She reaches behind her back and unhooks her bra.

It lands beside her dress.

And there they are. Two perfect, symmetrical triangles. Enticing me with their petite perfection.

"Do you want to touch my breasts?" she asks.

I do, but I don't.

"I thought you found fucking me to be a deplorable act?"

She shrugs.

"I just want to feel a bit of love before I die."

Now she removes her knickers.

An entirely shaved pussy stares back at me, wanting to be touched, wanting my cock, wanting me to thrust and pound it until she screams out in pain or pleasure, either one I do not care.

She gets to her knees.

She opens her mouth.

I am not about to risk that.

I am not about to be fooled.

So I approach her and I put my hand around her neck and I move her onto her back.

She puts her hands above her head and her chest stretches and her breasts fall succinctly to the side. A painting of exquisite beauty would not match the sight.

I undo my belt and I bring my stiff cock out and she looks at it and I move it lower.

"Turn me over," she says.

"What?"

"Turn me over. Do it like you always did. I want you to hurt me."

"What?"

"I want to feel the pain again. I want you to thrust it into me as hard as you can. I want to feel it on my insides."

I do as she wishes.

I turn her over.

I spread her legs.

And I thrust my cock in as hard as it will go, and as far inside of her as it will reach.

And I scream.

And I pass out.

BACK WHEN

Back when you were still asleep.

Back when I took the bleach and I put it in your breakfast.

Back when I left the bleach on the side, I knew I'd need a backup plan.

I knew you would not resist me.

It's your carnal sexuality that overrides your need to kill.

It's the only weapon I truly have against you.

You are attracted to my adolescent body so much it will outdo any wish you have to murder me.

You will get to the murder, yes, but first you will not miss up an opportunity for a final fuck.

I heard you get up. I heard you step out of the bed and wonder where I was.

And I knew I needed something else, just in case.

That's when I opened the cutlery drawer.

That's when I saw it.

Back when you were walking down the first set of stairs.

Back when I heard you so far off in such a big house.

Back when I decided to do whatever it took to survive.

I took the corkscrew from the drawer.

I felt its sharp, pointed, painful edge. A small circumference with a twisted screw that could pierce wood. Long, metal and twisted, that would push through a cork just as it could push through you.

I was wearing nothing but your shirt.

And it makes you want me.

So I took the corkscrew and I spread my legs and I reached inside of myself and I pushed it in.

It hurt, Gerry.

It really hurt.

I was dry and it scraped my insides, but I heard you approaching.

I heard you reach the bottom step.

Back when you paused to look around.

Back when you wondered where I was.

Back when you made your way toward the kitchen.

That was when I was reaching my fingers further, pushing further, and placing it so far in I knew it would not come out.

And you came in.

And you saw the bleach bottle I left out and I hated myself for it and I knew I was going to die.

But I knew I had a chance.

Back when you saw me as you spoke to the cops.

Back when you put me in the car.

Back when you knew you had me.

That was when I was resolved.

To death, or for one last fuck.

But this fuck would be the last fuck you ever gave me.

No more, Gerald.

No more.

You took the bait and you thrust in as deep and hard as you could, not just because I requested it, but because that's what you like to do.

Your face... When the long piece of metal, spiralling and sharp, went straight down your shaft... As you thrusted in as hard as you could and forced it through you...

I finally understood what it was you enjoyed so much about seeing someone's face in pain.

You like to hurt me.

And now I hurt you.

Those prickly edges caught you and you had to pull away and the blood fell out of me, but this time, it was not my blood that poured down my legs.

My legs were painted red, but it was not my paint.

It was yours, and you squirmed.

Back when I should have killed you.

Back when I took the knife.

Back when you passed out from the pain in an instant and I put the knife to your throat and pressed.

But I am not like you, Gerald.

I am not a killer.

Even you, the bastard who has destroyed me, has changed me for life, has given me trauma that I will never recover from – I could not.

Back when I put the tip against your throat and pleaded with myself to end it.

Back when I told myself you deserved it, that I wouldn't be put in prison for it.

Back when I realised you had so much money that your luck would find a way out of it.

So I dropped the knife.

And I looked at you for one final time.

A crotch soaked in blood. A sight so satisfying.

You'll never touch me again, Gerald.

Never.

I am going to run and not look back.

I am going to leave and never say a word.
I am going to be the burden that makes you worry every day.
Back when I thought keeping silent was the best thing to do.
Back when I watched you sleeping, just as I do now.
Back when I wished you dead, and now when I can't do it.
Goodbye, Gerald.
We will never meet again.
Back when I thought this to be true.
Back when I escaped.
Back when I didn't realise that you would never relent.
When I didn't know there was no goodbye.
The curtains have closed.
The sentence has ended.
The book has finished.
The final full stop is here, Gerald.
It's this one right now.
Back when I ran.
Back when I stopped crying.
Back when I never gave up.

39

WELL, that was a climax, wasn't it?
I mean, not for me, but for the story.
I guess that's the end then.
Goodbye.

40

————

THAT'S NOT REALLY good enough for you, though, is it?

If I left the story there you would be left wholly unsatisfied. You would take to the customer review section of whatever platform you have acquired this book through and write something such as *this book ended right where I did not want it to*, putting your opinion in writing so as to validate it somehow, writing with the self-entitlement all reviews, professional or otherwise, seem to have.

Chances are you are already going to take to the customer review section to complain about the violence or the sick and twisted and unethical management of the book's subject matter.

But I warned you about that in chapter one, did I not?

What, you thought I was kidding?

But that is not what I am addressing here. You have your opinion that you will undoubtedly express, and I could not care less.

I assume that there are other numerous unanswered questions I should address in this, the ultimate chapter of my first memoir, are there not?

I will attempt to guess the questions you wish to have answered, and I will do my best to address them – as a human mind can never deal with not knowing the answers.

That is why you invent gods, after all.

So my prediction is that you wish to know about the following, which I shall lay out here in a standard bullet point formatting:

- My dick
- Mark
- Lisa
- Officer Ian
- Flora

And we will start with the first of those subjects, the most important and valuable one of them all – *my dick*.

Well, I woke up in the field with a pool of blood around my crotch.

(And no Flora – but that is inevitably the last point on my bullet point list, so I will address it in good time. My appendage is a far more important matter than the petulant sexual deviant who, quite literally, fucked me over.)

I did attend a hospital, of course, not wanting to leave permanent damage to the one part of my body I truly cannot live without.

The hospital asked questions, and I gave them the answers they needed.

I was doing a prank to impress my friends at a party.

It was late and I was sweaty and it was enough to make them believe me.

They stitched me up and I'll be fine, so don't worry about me, dear voyeur, my dick will live to fuck another day.

Mark never turned up.

I mean, of course he wouldn't, a bunch of pigs ate him – but no one knows that but me and the soon-to-be-addressed Flora.

The police say they have not abandoned their investigation, but they are taking more and more resources away from it as they find the search for answers increasingly futile.

The family have since hired a private investigator to continue the investigation, that I have funded, who has also come up with very little. They thanked me greatly for supplying the money that allows them to retain their hope.

The mother spoke in a press conference, months after the disappearance, that she very much believes her son is alive, and will one day return home.

She remains a deluded imbecile.

Lisa's body was identified by myself, and the police confirmed that she drowned, and, after a few enquiries, and details of the depression she had been suffering from that I had falsely given them, they concluded that it was suicide.

The youths who stabbed Officer Ian Darling were never found, and his history of depression also led to the police believing it was suicide. However, they are still following leads and are yet to conclude the investigation. I have been contacted for further questioning following my statement, which was concluded to the police's satisfaction.

I have also donated money to a charity that helps people in the emergency services and armed forces that have depression.

And, finally, Flora.

Ah, Flora.

This is the one you want to know about, isn't it?

Well, in the weeks following her untimely getaway, no police ever showed up at my door, no journalist ever printed a story about me, and no claims were made that would stop everyone believing I am the charitable billionaire that they know I am.

She quite evidently seems to have disappeared.

But I have not given up hope.

Yes, she has remained quiet, most likely out of fear, or maybe as some kind of unspoken deal between us that, should she never speak of what happened, I will never come after her.

My dear voyeur, I must tell you, that I do not agree to such a deal.

See, these people who claim that they were abused, as they term it, by people of similar relations, rarely come clean straight away.

It is in the years, or even decades, afterwards, in which the revolutions are made.

And I have no doubt that, someday, should she live, I will get that knock on my door.

I will get that journalist writing their article.

And I will get that charitable billionaire reputation besmirched.

And that is why I cannot allow her to live.

And that, my dear, dear, voyeur, my acquaintance through prose, my friend of no face – is why I hunt her like a farmer hunts a fox.

I track her and I search for her and I go everywhere I think she will go.

Not for revenge.

She did what she did because she was cunning, because she learnt from the best, and my penis survived the inevitable trauma she caused it.

It is because I wish to carry on doing this for as long as I live, and I will not do this from a prison cell.

And, as long she is alive, I am in that prison cell.

Not literally, of course, my house is far grander than incarceration, as you well know.

But I cannot kill and I cannot feed my needs until she is caught, so I know that I am safe from unwanted consequences.

And now, dear voyeur, I would like to stop addressing you in the final words of this memoir.

I would, instead, like to address Flora.

My darling, darling Flora.

Flora, to which I gave so much adoration, only to be met with hate and resistance.

I don't care where you are.

I don't care what you are doing.

And I don't care who you are fucking.

I will come after you.

I will get you.

And I will tear your limbs off and expose your insides.

I promise you, Flora, with everything I have.

Wherever you are.

Whatever you are thinking.

I will find you, Flora.

I swear it.

I will find you.

JOIN RICK WOOD'S READER'S GROUP...

And get **Roses Are Red So Is Your Blood** for free!

Join at **www.rickwoodwriter.com/sign-up**

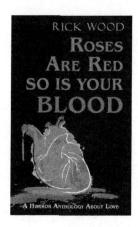

HAVE YOU READ SHUTTER HOUSE?

The book that inspired this prequel...

BLOOD SPLATTER BOOKS
SHUTTER HOUSE
RICK WOOD
18+

BLOOD
SPLATTER
BOOKS

PSYCHO
B*TCHES

RICK WOOD

18+

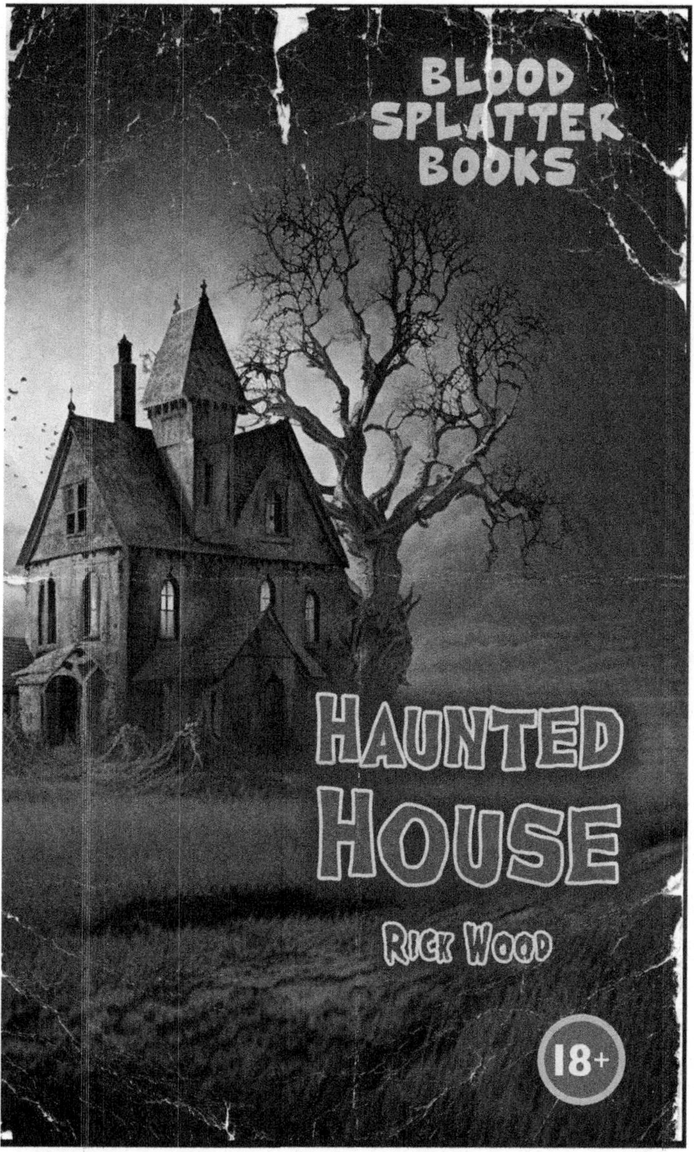
BLOOD SPLATTER BOOKS
HAUNTED HOUSE
RICK WOOD
18+

BLOOD
SPLATTER
BOOKS

HOME
INVASION

RICK WOOD

18+

BLOOD
SPLATTER
BOOKS

WOMAN
SCORNED

RICK WOOD

18+

ALSO BY RICK WOOD...

BOOK ONE IN THE SENSITIVES SERIES

THE
SENSITIVES

RICK WOOD

BOOK ONE IN THE ROGUE EXORCIST SERIES

THE HAUNTING
OF EVIE MEYERS

RICK WOOD

Printed in Great Britain
by Amazon

37567198R00169